Rodale

The Mystery
of the 13th Coin

The Mystery of the 13th Coin

Mary Gordon Kerr

illustrated by Jeff Welch

High Tide Publishing, LLC

HIGHTIDE
PUBLISHING,LLC

This is a work of fiction. With the exception of the mention of a well-known historical figure, all characters, events and dialogue are from the author's imagination and are not real. Where actual historical places and structures are part of the story, the dialogue and events surrounding those places is entirely fictional. Any resemblance to real people, living or dead, is coincidental.

Text copyright © 2008 Mary Gordon Kerr
Illustrations copyright © 2008 Jeff Welch

For information on the publisher, visit hightidepublishing.com.

ISBN 978-0-9802010-1-7

Printed in the United States of America   First Edition

High Tide Publishing, LLC

For the students of Ms. Hopkins' 2nd Grade Class
2005-2006 at Mount Pleasant Academy,
whose enthusiasm and creativity
influenced this story

Dear Reader,

The students in Ms. Hopkins' 2nd grade class joined me in the writing of this story from the very first chapter. Each week I met with the class for feedback. In our time together they listened carefully to each new chapter. We discussed plot possibilities and character development. No idea was too far fetched to be heard. I had a wonderful time crafting the story and I am excited about sharing it with you. My special thanks to Anne Peyre, Anna Katherine, Bronte, Brianna, Cailin, Destiny, Flynn, Gracie, Harris, Harrison, Jelissa, Lauren, Mokie, Nick, Sydney, Tyler and Sue Hopkins. Now fasten your seatbelt as you enter the adventure of "The Mystery of the 13th Coin."

Mary Gordon Ken

Contents

CHAPTER
1

Kick the Stone Home

Nothing really exciting ever happened to Trip Traveler. Every day he had the same routine. He went to school, came home, went to soccer practice, did his homework, ate and went to bed. He liked his life. He always knew what to expect, and that was good as far as he was concerned.

But something different had happened today. He put his hand in his pocket and wrapped his fingers around the strange silver coin he had found wedged under a rock near the old abandoned house he always walked by on his way home from school. He had found the coin there quite by accident.

Every day for the past two weeks, Trip and his friend, Sam, had searched for a stone in the school yard during recess. They had used big ones, small ones, flat ones and round ones. They had decided that the medium-sized round rocks worked the best. After school, they would take turns kicking the stone toward their neighborhood and see how long they could go without kicking the stone off the path. So far, they hadn't made it farther than the basketball courts on Center Street.

But today, just as they passed the Post Office and rounded the corner next to the Old Miller Place, Trip kicked the rock a little too hard. It bounced off the path and under a gap in an old wooden fence that kept trespassers from bothering the old abandoned mansion.

"Wait a minute," Trip said. "I can get that."

"That's okay," Sam answered. "We can get another one tomorrow."

"No, really, I can reach it," Trip said as he moved over close to the fence and lay flat on his belly. He stretched his arm through the same gap where he'd seen his rock disappear. With the palm of his hand open wide, Trip patted the ground as far as he could reach in every direction. He didn't want to lose his rock. It was smooth and white, almost round and the best rock they had found since last Tuesday.

"Do you feel it?" Sam asked.

"Not yet."

"Let me see," Sam said as he crawled up next to Trip and plopped down on his belly too. "Move your hand, Trip. Let me see."

Sam peered under the rotting fence. He strained

to see something besides the tangled mess of tall green weeds. He pressed his cheek harder into the dirt distorting his face. "I can't see a thing," he said in frustration. Just then, a glint of sunlight reflected off something shiny just to the right of Sam's hand. "Oh, hold on. I might see something," he said as he lifted his head and strained to reach toward what he had seen.

"It's probably the rock," Trip said. "It is really white. Let me see if I can reach it."

Sam pulled his arm back as Trip flattened himself to the ground again and pushed his arm through the gap under the fence. "I do feel a big rock," he said, "but it's not ours." Just as he was about to give up, Trip said, "Hey, I've got something, but it's stuck under that rock." Trip began to wiggle the object back and forth until it started to move. With a final tug, it broke free. Trip wrapped his fingers around it and pulled his hand back through the fence.

CHAPTER
2

The Coin

Trip uncurled his dirt-smudged fingers to look at his newfound treasure. "Cool," he said. With his elbow he rubbed off some dirt with his shirt sleeve and then turned and held his hand out in front of Sam. "You're not going to believe this! Look what I found."

The object in Trip's hand was a coin, but it was unlike any coin he had ever seen before. It was big – almost as big as the bottom of a bottle of water. It was a silver color and Trip believed that it must indeed be made of real silver. He could tell from looking at it that it was very old. "Very old and very valuable," he thought. It was heavy, like he assumed a real silver coin should be, and it had strange markings and words that Trip did not understand. That in itself made his discovery all the more exciting.

"Whoa! What do you think that is?" Sam asked.

Trip shrugged his shoulders, "I don't know."

Sam rubbed his thumb over the face of the coin

and squinted as he studied the treasure in Trip's hand. "I wonder if anybody is missing that?"

"I doubt it," Trip said confidently. "That old place has been boarded up for years. You know what they say anyway, right? Finders keepers ..."

Sam finished Trip's sentence with him, "Losers weepers."

Trip grinned broadly, "Guess we're the finders then."

"I sure wouldn't know who to return it to," Sam said. "So I guess it is ours."

The idea of kicking the stone along the path had long been forgotten and for the rest of the way home, Trip and Sam talked excitedly about where the coin might have come from and argued about which boy would take the coin to his house. It was finally decided that since Trip was the one who had actually pulled the coin free, Trip would be the one to take the coin home that afternoon.

When he sat down at his desk under the loft bed in his room to do his homework, Trip could hardly concentrate at all. His mind wandered as he read a story he'd been assigned to read and he didn't know the answers to any of the story review questions. It had taken him twice as long as usual to do his math worksheet and he still hadn't made sentences with his spelling words. He

Mary Gordon Kerr

kept stopping to stick his hand in his pocket so he could touch the silver coin that lay heavy on his leg. Every now and then he'd pull it out and look at it again. By now he was familiar with the design on the coin. On one side there was a picture of a chain making a circle around what appeared to be a fountain or a wave. Trip felt sure that it was some kind of water. The chain came together at the bottom of the circle with an old-fashioned lock like Trip imagined might be on an old pirate treasure chest. The other side of the coin had letters that made up words Trip couldn't read. The words "veritas in aqua est" curved around the top arc of the coin. The number 13 was below that with what looked like wings coming out of each side of the number. The word "libertas" was written under the number.

Trip didn't know what any of it meant except that he'd probably have to stay in from recess the next day for coming to school without his homework finished. His mom had called him for dinner, and after that it was time for his shower and then bed. His mom and dad were pretty serious about his bedtime since school started so early. He put his books away, patted his pocket just to make sure the coin was still there and went to join his family for dinner.

CHAPTER

3

Truth is in Water

At the dinner table, Trip pulled out the coin to show his parents. He told them the whole story about how he and Sam had lost their stone under the fence and had found the silver coin wedged under a rock.

"I've been trying to figure out what the stuff on the coin means," Trip said. "Like the number 13 with wings? That's weird. And the chain around the water – I don't know what that means either."

Trip traced his pointer finger under the writing and read aloud, "veritas in aqua est" and "libertas." "I'm not sure what that means either, but I wonder if aqua has something to do with water. You know, like Aqua Man or aquarium. And then there's the water here inside the chain." He pointed to the coin.

"I bet that's right," his Dad said. "The writing looks like Latin."

"Interesting, " his Mom chimed in. "I took Latin in school. Veritas means truth – like in our word verify.

And Libertas means freedom."

"Like our word 'liberty'," Mr. Traveler said nodding his head.

"So truth in water is?" asked Trip.

"Well, in Latin, the action word is always at the end of the sentence," Mrs. Traveler said. "So what it seems to say is 'truth is in water' and then down below the wings here, the word 'libertas' means 'freedom'," she said as she pointed below the number 13 on the back of the coin.

"Hm-m-m," Trip said thoughtfully. "Well, I'm not sure what it all means, but I'll at least write that down."

"You know, when I was a teenager, the people who owned that house just picked up and left town. It has been abandoned ever since," said Mr. Traveler. "A lot of guys thought the house was haunted."

"People still say that," Trip said. "But I never really believed it."

By the look Mrs. Traveler gave her husband, Trip knew his mother didn't want to talk about it any more. Even though he was almost ten years old, he knew she thought too much talk about haunted houses would give him bad dreams.

After dinner, Trip got in the bathtub with the coin in his hand. He carefully stepped into the water and sat down using just one hand for support. He was trying to keep the coin dry. He had decided that, if the house was haunted or magic, getting the coin wet may reveal some sort of secret message and he wanted to be sure he was paying close attention when he put it in the water. As he held the coin on its edges between his finger and his thumb, he slowly lowered it into the water. When nothing seemed to change, he turned it over and studied the other side as well. Still nothing happened.

Trip was disappointed. He had hoped he was on to something with his idea of getting the coin wet. When he got out of the tub, he vigorously rubbed both sides of the coin with his towel and waited expectantly for something to happen. "After all", he thought, "isn't that how a genie gets out of its magic lamp?" Still nothing happened. After he put on his pajamas, he put the coin in the sink and turned the water on as hot as it would go. He watched the water splash off the surface of the coin, hoping the water temperature would reveal some sort of secret. Still nothing. Then he filled up his toothbrush rinse cup with water and began to dunk the coin as he counted. One, two, three … all the way to 13. Still nothing.

That night Trip went to bed believing that perhaps the coin he had found was not as special as he had thought it was. The discovery had been exciting, he thought, but maybe the adventure was over. As in answer to his own thoughts he sleepily mumbled, "I hope not." He then drifted off to sleep with the coin safely tucked under his pillow.

CHAPTER
4
Emily

"I don't think we should give up so easily, Trip," Sam said the next day at school. Trip had told Sam about all the events of the previous evening concerning the coin. "Even if it doesn't have some secret message, it probably has a cool story and it's got to at least be worth something."

"Yeah, you're probably right," Trip said. He was glad he had Sam as a friend. He was always looking on the bright side of things and Trip liked that.

"Let's meet at the library after school. Maybe we can find out something about the coin or that spooky old house on the internet."

Trip agreed to meet Sam at the library at 3 o'clock.

At 2:55 Trip was sitting on a low stone wall outside the library waiting for Sam who'd had to go back to his classroom for a book he'd left in his desk. He was flipping the coin in the air with his thumb and catching it.

For about the tenth time, he flipped it up in the air and as it came down, it slipped through his fingers and clinked onto the pavement below the wall where he was sitting. Before he could jump down to retrieve it, his friend, Emily, who had been coming up the walk, leaned over and picked it up.

"That's mine," Trip said with just a hint of panic in his voice.

"I know," Emily said. She smiled as she looked at him. "What are you so jumpy about Trip Traveler? I was just picking it up for you."

"Right. Thanks," he said sheepishly. "It's just kind of important to me. That's all."

Emily held the coin in her hand and studied it. "That's unusual. Where'd it come from?"

Trip wasn't sure if he should say. He and Sam hadn't talked about whether or not they should tell anyone else about the coin. It wasn't that he didn't like Emily. He did. They'd been in the same class in second grade and had sat next to each other the whole year. Although he hadn't told anybody, he thought she was the coolest girl he'd ever met. She was really pretty and smart too, but she was also tough. When the kids played kickball during recess, the team captains always picked Emily before they even picked him.

"Earth to Trip," Emily was saying.

"Oh, sorry," Trip said. "I was just thinking."

"You can't remember where it came from?" she said with a giggle in her voice.

Trip felt foolish. "Yeah. I just wasn't sure if I should tell you," he said. "It's really none of your business."

"Oh," she said, sounding a little hurt. "Fine, suit yourself. See you at school Trip," she said as she flipped the coin back to him.

Trip felt a twinge of guilt as he watched her walk away. He was about to call after her when Sam rounded the corner. "Hey Buddy. Sorry you had to wait."

"Oh, Hey," said Trip.

Sam put his hand on Trip's shoulder as they started up the walk. "Any new ideas?" he asked.

"Not really," Trip answered. He was still feeling guilty about his exchange with Emily.

"Well, let's see what we can find out on the internet," Sam said as they entered the library.

For about half an hour, Trip and Sam entered words into the search engine on the computer. They typed in "Miller Place" and found about a dozen sites related to a town in New York called Miller Place, a web page for Miller Place High School, various hotel websites and one charity home page, but nothing about the abandoned house they called "the Old Miller Place". They typed in "magic coins" and found countless sites on where to buy coins to use for magic tricks. They typed in at least a half dozen other words, but still couldn't get anywhere with their research. As Trip leaned back in his chair, let out a frustrated sigh and ran both hands through his hair, he spotted her out of the corner of his eye.

There was Emily -- smart, beautiful, tough Emily surfing the internet with ease. She was clicking and taking down notes, nodding and printing out more notes. Sam followed Trip's gaze and saw her too.

"Hm-m-m," said Sam. "I wonder if Emily could help us? She knows a lot of stuff."

"Yeah, she does, but ..."

Before Trip could finish his sentence, Sam was already walking toward her. As Sam spoke to her, Emily looked in Trip's direction. Trip's eyes darted away from her and he felt his face get hot. He was embarrassed for the way he'd spoken to her earlier.

Emily pushed her chair back to stand up and followed Sam back to where Trip was sitting.

"Hi Trip," Emily said with a triumphant smile. "Sam says you have a coin you would like me to take a look at."

CHAPTER

5

A Clue

The boys told Emily all that had happened since they first kicked their rock off the path the previous day. She listened with great interest and interrupted only to ask a few questions. They told her that they had come to the library to search the internet for some kind of clue as to where the coin had come from and anything else interesting about it.

After they had filled her in on all the search words they had used so far, Sam said, "Trip thinks it might be magic."

"Well, I said it was possible," Trip said and then quickly added, "but probably not." He didn't want Emily to think he was weird for believing the coin might lead to something really unusual. It was just a coin, after all.

"I think that would be a wonderful adventure!" Emily said. Trip smiled and thought to himself how much he really did like Emily. She was fun to be around and he was glad Sam had asked her to help. She pulled a chair up next to Trip's in front of the computer screen and said, "Let's see what we can find."

As she typed, she explained that she was looking for the Preservation Society web page for Mount Pleasant, the coastal town where they lived. "They protect places like the Old Miller Place and won't let anybody tear them down," she said. As she scrolled through a list of protected places listed on the web site, Trip exclaimed, "There it is!"

Emily clicked on the link and in less than a minute, a photograph of what was labeled as "Miller Plantation" filled the screen. In the picture, the house was in much better condition and didn't look very spooky at all.

Emily began to read out loud as Trip and Sam looked over her shoulder, "Miller plantation was built in 1767 by a man named Charles Miller. At the time the house was built, Charles Miller was an independently wealthy newcomer to the area. A very private man, mystery surrounded him. Very little was known about his family or how he had earned his fortune. It was rumored that Miller had sailed with the notorious Pirate called Blackbeard under the name Digger Miller. His association with Edward Teach, who was also known as Blackbeard, is undocumented."

"A Pirate?" Trip said in awe. "Do you think that

could have something to do with the coin?" He asked.

"That's so cool!" Sam said. "Why didn't we know about that?"

"Wow." Emily said. "This could get interesting. Let's see what else it says."

Emily ran her finger down the screen as she skimmed through the information there. "It looks like no one's lived there since the 1980s when two of the Miller children who lived there disappeared mysteriously from the house," she said. "It says here that their family thought the house was haunted. They signed the deed over to the town and haven't looked back since."

"Does it say anything about treasure?" Trip asked.

"Yeah, what about the coin?" Sam added.

"No, it doesn't mention the coin," she said.

Trip leaned in closer to the computer. "What's that?" he asked as he squinted at a drawing on the screen and moved the mouse back and forth to point it out. "It looks like a little map of the Miller place."

"Yeah," Sam said. "Look, this is the big house and then there's this smaller house behind it labeled 'kitchen' and then this round thing over here is an old well, I think," he said pointing to the diagram. Sam clicked the mouse on "print screen" and said, "This might come in handy."

As they were waiting for the map to print out, Trip scrolled down to the next screen. As he did, Emily leaned toward him, reached across his chest and pointed at the screen. "Look," she said excitedly. "There's a picture of that old well that's on the map."

All three leaned in close to the screen and studied it. Emily began to read the caption. "It says that there is an inscription carved around the top of the well, but that historians have been unable to determine the meaning of its message."

"Here's the message," Trip said pointing to the screen.

All three read in unison. "To set it free you must let go, Time will fly, away you'll go."

Emily sat back amazed. "Guys, I don't know what it means yet, but I think we have found our first real clue."

Trip and Sam both let out a celebratory yell and high-fived each other. Sam tousled Emily's hair and said, "You *go* girl."

The Librarian walked directly toward them with a stern look. She held her finger up to her lips indicating that they should be quiet. Trip shrugged his shoulders apologetically and mouthed the word, "sorry."

He turned back around toward Emily and said,

"Forget about what I said. This is definitely your business now. Come on guys, we have a mystery to solve."

CHAPTER

6

Waiting for Saturday

The three friends decided that if they were going to discover anything interesting about the coin, they were going to have to explore the place where Trip and Sam had found it – the Old Miller Place. Because the following day was Saturday, they decided to meet in front of the Post Office at nine o'clock the next morning. Just before they went home, Sam pulled the crumpled map of Miller Plantation out of his pocket and handed it to Trip. "Don't forget to bring this and the coin tomorrow," he said as Trip stuffed the map in his pocket.

When Trip got home, he unfolded the map and carefully smoothed it out on top of his desk. He hunched over it and studied the diagram on the map. He dug into his pocket and pulled out the heavy silver coin. He thought if he looked at the coin and the map together, he might notice something new. His eyes fell on the wave on the face of the coin, and he thought about the words "veritas in aqua est" which he thought meant, "truth is in water."

He glanced back at the map in hopes of seeing some sort of water source like a stream, or a pond there. He knew that the house was less than a block from the harbor, but he didn't notice a body of water on the map itself. Then it hit him. The clue they found when they were at the library was on a well.

"Of course," he thought. "If that's a well, then I bet it has water," He turned the piece of paper over that had the printout of the map on it. He was pretty sure that Emily had scribbled down the words that were carved around the top of the well. Yes, there they were. Trip read them out loud, "To set it free you must let go, time will fly, away you'll go." He circled the well on the map with a red marker and then folded it back up. He could hardly wait for Saturday to come.

On Saturday morning, Trip met Sam in front of his house and the two of them walked toward the Post Office where they would meet Emily. Trip carried a camouflaged backpack and Sam had a small garden spade.

"What's that for?" Trip asked as he looked at the little shovel.

"We may need to dig around to find something. There may be more coins where this one came from," Sam said.

"Okay," Trip said. "You want to put it in my

backpack?"

"Sure. What else is in there?" Sam asked.

"Exploration supplies," Trip said as he stopped walking and put his pack on the ground. He opened the zipper wide to show Sam its contents. "You know, flashlights, matches, a notebook and pen, binoculars, a compass, my slingshot, a pocketknife, my scout canteen with water and a few snacks."

"Good," Sam said, nodding his head in approval. "What about the map and the coin?"

Trip patted his leg where his pocket was. "Oh, I'm keeping those in my pocket just in case I get separated from my backpack."

Trip zipped up his pack, swung it over one shoulder and the two boys continued on their way. In about ten minutes, they were in view of the Post Office and could see Emily standing out front. She waved as they approached. She was dressed in faded jeans with a small tear in the knee and a lime green hoodie sweatshirt.

"Hey guys," she said as they both gave her a small wave. "I thought you'd never get here. I'm so excited."

"Me too," they both said in unison. "Jinx," they said together again and then looked at each other and laughed.

"Well, what are we waiting for?" Emily said.

"Let's get going."

CHAPTER
7

Barking Up the Oak Tree

Trip, Sam and Emily walked around the perimeter of the old Miller place looking for a way to get on the other side of the fence. Climbing the fence would not have been much of a problem, but they didn't want to draw attention to themselves. On two sides of the property, the fence was just a few feet from the sidewalk and then the road. They crouched down and ran along the portion of the fence that backed up to a house that overlooked the harbor.

"That oak tree has a limb hanging down over the fence," Sam said pointing to a tree in the yard of the harbor house.

"Yeah, but we'll have to move away from the fence and into their yard to get in the tree," Emily said. "We might get caught."

"Come on," Sam said. "Adventures have risks... right buddy?" Sam said looking right at Trip.

"Uh, right," Trip said hesitantly. He didn't think going a little further into a neighbor's yard was that big a risk, but he didn't want to seem like he was taking sides this early in their exploration.

"Let's go," Sam said as he ran toward the tree. He motioned for his friends to follow him.

Trip and Emily ran after him. When they got to the trunk of the old oak tree, they saw that the tree was about five feet in diameter and that the first foothold in the tree was higher than it had appeared.

"Give me a boost," Sam said as he lifted one foot against the massive tree trunk and reached for some sort of hand holds with his fingers. Trip squatted down, laced his fingers together to make a step for Sam's foot and hoisted him up to where Sam could shimmy into a trough of the tree near the branch they wanted to reach. He had just taken Emily's foot into his hands to boost her up when a dog came around the house and spotted them. The dog stopped and growled, let out several deep barks and then, barking with all of his might, ran toward the tree. Emily screamed, "Trip, hurry!"

With the extra adrenaline of the moment, Trip boosted Emily high and then desperately tried to scramble up the tree trunk himself. He took a few steps back and started to run up the tree trunk yelling, "Help me!" He reached his hands as far up the trunk as he could manage. To his relief, he felt a hand clasp his wrist. He looked up and saw Sam straining to pull him up. Emily was reaching toward him also.

"Give me your other hand, Trip," she said. Trip reached up as far as he could with his other hand and she grabbed it. Both his friends continued to pull as he frantically moved his feet up the trunk. Once he was secured in the tree, he looked down at the dog. It wasn't quite as big or fierce as it had sounded, but Trip had no doubt that the dog had meant business. With his front paws on the trunk of the tree, he glared up at Trip with bared teeth, growling, barking and then growling again.

"Whew," Trip sighed. "That was close. Thanks, guys."

"Are you okay, Trip?" Emily said.

Before he could answer, Sam said, "You should've seen your face, Trip! You were really scared."

"I wasn't scared," Trip said with more confidence than he felt. "Now, please move so we can get on with this."

Emily and Sam exchanged glances and moved out of Trip's way as best they could in their small perch in the tree. Trip carefully moved out onto the limb that led over the fence into the Miller property. He crawled across the wide limb on his hands and knees until he was over the fence and just about six feet off the ground. He crouched on his feet and jumped to the ground. Sam and Emily followed closely behind him.

When all three were safely on the ground, Trip said, "We should look for another way out while we're in here. No reason to make him mad." Trip tilted his head toward the barking dog on the other side of the fence.

Emily and Sam both laughed. "That's a good plan," Sam said.

Trip pulled the computer print-out of the map from his pocket. "Okay," he said. "Let's figure out where we are."

CHAPTER
8
The Hand

Trip looked at the map and then looked up to take in the landscape around him. The only readily identifiable structure was the old mansion itself. The problem was that the house and surrounding property were so overgrown with weeds and vines it was hard to pick out a path to the house or to locate the other structures they wanted to find. They were, of course, especially interested in the old well, but now they were unsure they would be able to find it at all.

"This is going to be harder than I thought," said Emily.

"My pocket knife may not help us here," Trip said with a laugh.

"You don't have a machete in there, do you?" Sam said with a crooked grin as he motioned toward the backpack.

"I wish," Trip answered.

"Maybe we should make our way to the house,

and then find our bearings from there," Emily suggested.

Trip and Sam agreed, and the three friends began trudging their way through the tangled mess toward the house. It was still early and they had plenty of time to explore. After a few minutes, Trip was the first to reach a back wall of the house near a rear door.

"Try the door, Trip," Sam called ahead.

Trip moved along the wall and wiggled the rusty handle.

"It's locked," he said.

"Great," Sam said sarcastically.

"Are you sure?" Emily asked as she pushed a vine aside and came up behind him.

She moved close to the door and put her hand on the knob. She tried to turn it, but it wouldn't budge. With her hand still on the knob, she turned her head toward Trip and Sam.

She started to say, "Maybe we should try another ...", but before she could finish the thought, the door jerked open, pulling Emily off balance and into the doorway. Emily screamed and then, as quickly as it had opened, the door shut again, except now, Emily was gone.

"Emily!" Sam yelled.

Trip ran to the door and tried to open it. He threw his shoulder against the door repeatedly, trying to get it to budge, but it was hopelessly stuck.

"Help me!" he yelled at Sam whose face had turned completely white. He looked like he might get sick.

Still frozen where he stood, Sam quietly uttered, "Did you see it?"

Trip stopped and looked at him. "See what?" he asked.

"That hand," Sam whispered.

"What?"

"A hand," he said. "A hand pulled Emily through the door."

Trip's eyes grew wide and more frantic. He turned back toward the door and began to pound on it. Sam joined him and they both pounded their fists on the door, yelling as loud as they could.

"Let us in!"

"Give her back!"

"Open the door!"

"Emily!"

After several minutes they stopped yelling. Trip sank to the ground and leaned against the wall of the old house.

"What are we going to do?" Trip said, leaning his forehead on his hands. His voice was almost hoarse from yelling.

Sam was beginning to get his composure back and was trying hard to look confident for his friend.

"We're going to find another way in. That's what we're going to do. We're going to get her back and find out what this is all about." He reached down to grab Trip's hand and pulled him to his feet. "Come on. We've got to hurry."

On the other side of the door, everything happened so quickly, that before Emily saw anything, she felt herself sliding through a winding tunnel. The fright of being pulled into the door must have caused her to black out, because the next thing she knew, she was sliding. Down, down, down she slid. All of a sudden the slide disappeared beneath her and she was in mid-air. She tried to scream, but couldn't make any sound come out of her mouth. Suddenly, she landed with a thud on a pile of soft cushions. When she opened her eyes, she gasped. She couldn't believe what she saw. She opened her mouth in amazement and whispered to herself, "Someone lives here!"

CHAPTER
9

The Secret Room

Emily couldn't believe her eyes. She pushed herself up on the pile of cushions and looked around the room. There was an old wooden table with two chairs. A big piece of paper that was curled up on the edges was spread across the table with a rock, a book and a pewter mug holding it down on three of the corners. A small candle that was lit had burned about half way down and was dripping wax onto the base of a tarnished brass candlestick holder. Under the table was an old worn looking oriental rug that ran over to the edge of a bed that appeared to have been slept in quite recently. Mounted on the walls were several torches that were also lit and were casting a flickering light around the small room. Every now and then, the flames would dim as a draft swept through the room.

Emily timidly called out, "Hello? Is anyone here? Hello?"

Emily couldn't see or hear anyone, but she still sat

motionless, watching and waiting. She was too frightened to move.

***

Outside the house, Trip and Sam were looking for a way in. Sam was trying to pry open a window near the ground.

"It won't budge," he grunted as he strained to open it.

"Do you think we should break it?" Trip said as he looked around for a heavy rock or stick to throw through the window.

"No. That'll just draw attention to where we are," Sam said. "Let's go on around the house and see what we can find."

When they reached the front of the house, Trip said, "We should at least *try* the front door," he said. "Who knows? Maybe that's our way in."

Sam agreed and the two boys crouched down and tried to run undetected toward the front porch. The door was partially obscured by vines and overgrown bushes that had overtaken much of the porch area. As Sam climbed the old wooden steps, a rotten board gave way under his foot.

"My foot is stuck," he whispered loudly to Trip.

Trip carefully came up and saw that Sam's whole

foot had gone through the rotten piece of wood and was completely stuck. Trip leaned over, gripped Sam's leg with both hands and pulled. The top of Sam's foot hit hard against the rotten boards, but would not break free.

"Ouch," Sam called out.

"Sorry," Trip said sarcastically. "I was just trying to help."

"Well, it didn't help," Sam shot back.

"Okay. Just calm down," Trip answered. "Let me see if I can untie your shoe lace when you pull your foot up."

As Sam pulled his foot up, Trip reached into the hole and pulled the bow loose. "I got it," he said. "Now just pull your foot out of the shoe."

Sam wiggled his foot and, after just a minimal effort, his foot slid out of his shoe and out of the hole. He tried to reach down to get his shoe out, but it had fallen down to where he couldn't reach it. "Great," he said with disgust. "Now I've got to rescue Emily with just one shoe."

While all this was happening, a hand pulled a curtain back ever so slightly from a window next to the front door. Two eyes were watching the boys argue and struggle with the shoe, but by the time Trip turned his attention back to the door, the stranger was gone.

"Look at this," Trip said as he carefully moved up to the porch. "A big door mat. That's weird. No one has lived here for a really long time, right?"

"The mat has probably been here for a long time too," Sam said.

Trip stepped on the mat and up to the door to try the handle. "Locked," he said.

"Let's try it together," suggested Sam. Both boys grabbed the door handle at the same time and braced themselves on the mat under their feet. Suddenly, there was a loud creaking noise. The mat gave way, swinging down on hinges that had been hidden under the door frame. Now the boys found themselves plunging into darkness.

Trip and Sam yelled and tried to stop themselves from falling, but their momentum sent them twisting and sliding further and further down.

***

Emily heard the commotion above her. The yelling, thumping and bumping grew closer and closer. She turned toward the noise and clamored out of the spot where she was sitting just as Trip and then Sam tumbled onto the pillows where she had landed earlier.

"Trip! Sam!" she exclaimed. "Where'd you come from?"

"Emily?" Trip said. "Are you okay?"

Sam looked around and said, "What is all this?"

CHAPTER

10

Surprised

Now that they were together again, the three friends were feeling more confident than they had the few moments before Trip and Sam came hurdling down the tunnel under the front door mat. They decided to get up and have a look around. They moved over toward the table where the candle was still burning next to the old paper they had seen lying there.

"It's a map!" Emily exclaimed.

"Yeah, but a map of what?" Trip added.

All three leaned in closer to try and make sense of the map.

"It looks sort of like a maze or something over here," Sam said pointing to a portion of the map on the lower right hand side of the paper.

Trip pulled the Library computer print-out of Miller Plantation from his pocket and unfolded it on the table next to the big map. "Wait just a minute," he said.

"What?" Emily asked impatiently.

"Look at this," he said. "This part of the map over here looks a whole lot like our map." He patted the left side of the map with his fingertips. "Look," he said as he circled something on the map with his finger. "That's got to be the well right here. But what's all that?" He said pointing to the maze-like drawing Sam had pointed out a moment earlier.

A low raspy voice answered, "They're underground tunnels."

Sam jumped, turned toward the voice and assumed a fighting stance he'd learned at karate lessons. Emily screamed, sat down on the floor and covered her head with her hands and arms. Trip was so startled he not only yelled, but fell backwards over one of the chairs around the table knocking it to the ground. He looked up from where he had fallen and said, "Leave us alone."

Standing before them was a man. It was difficult to tell how old he was because he had a red braided beard and a dirt smudged face that looked weathered, like a person who spends too much time in the sun. His eyes were pale blue and intense. He had on grey pants with several nicks and tears, a shirt that was probably once white and a long black coat that fell just above his knees. He wore tall boots and smelled worse than any of the children thought was humanly possible.

The man laughed a hearty laugh and said in an English accent, "Well now. If you wanted to be left alone, you shouldn't have gone snooping about."

Emily had uncovered her head and was beginning to recover from the initial shock of the stranger's arrival. "What do you want with us?" she asked defensively.

"I believe this young man has possession of something I need," the stranger said as he stared directly at Trip. Trip felt his neck and cheeks grow hot under the intense gaze of the strange man. He didn't know what to do. He felt sure that the man was referring to the coin in his pocket, but was afraid to admit that he had it. Trip picked up his backpack and tossed it at the man's feet. "Everything I brought is in there," Trip said. "I hope you find what you're looking for. Just let us go."

"You know what I'm looking for," he growled. "I'm looking for the coin that will get me back to the time I came from. Once I get there, I can find the other magic coins old Digger buried in these tunnels. Once I have all 13, the greatest treasure will be mine."

The stranger grabbed the pack, reached his hand into the front pocket, seemed satisfied and started to leave. "Wait," Emily said. Sam and Trip both stared hard at her. "What?" she said as she exchanged glances with them. "I have a question."

The man turned and looked at her.

"Why not explore the tunnels under Digger's house here and now?" she asked.

"Good question young lady," he answered. He patted the backpack. "I took this magic coin and that map from a couple of kids who came snooping around. They had found the coin with the flying 13 and the map in an old wooden box hidden behind some loose bricks in this very house in the year nineteen hundred and eighty-six. This was very odd considering the present time was seventeen hundred and sixty-eight. The 13 on the coin, they said, was for the 13th hour of the day. I stole it, and on the 13th hour of the day it brought me here."

"Did you find the coins?" she asked excitedly. She seemed to have forgotten where she was and who she was talking to.

"No I did not," he bellowed. "The tunnels no longer exist. They were destroyed when those two snooping children disappeared from here. For some reason, I arrived in a different time than the children had left. I have only been here a few months."

"Long enough to set up some pretty mean booby traps," Sam said.

The man ignored the comment.

"Why didn't you return to the time you came from

when you couldn't get in the tunnels?" Trip asked. He was also getting so absorbed in the story he had forgotten about the danger he'd felt moments earlier.

"I lost the coin when I went looking for food and digging tools," he said. "I couldn't risk being seen in the daylight, so my search for the coin was limited to the cover of darkness."

Emily was about to ask another question when the man held up his hand and yelled, "Enough! The 13th hour approaches and I must return." He grabbed the backpack and a torch from the wall and disappeared through a door near the bed.

CHAPTER
11
I'm In

As the strange man disappeared from view, Sam looked at Trip with a quizzical stare. "I thought you said you put the coin in your pocket just in case ..."

Trip interrupted him, "In case I got separated from my pack?"

"Yeah," Sam said. "But Old Man Pickle Breath out there thinks he has the coin."

"Right," Trip answered matter-of-factly with a slight smile on his lips.

Emily grabbed his arm impatiently. "Out with it, Trip. What's going on?"

"Okay, okay," he said. "But we have to hurry, because I think he'll be back."

"Why do you think he'll be back?" Sam asked with caution in his voice.

"Because he only thinks he has the right coin," Trip said. "When I was packing my backpack, I found a souvenir coin I got when I went with my family to Atlantis in the Bahamas last summer. It was about the same size and weight and I kind of thought we might be able to use it for something."

"For what, exactly?" Emily asked.

"I don't know," he said defensively. "I guess I thought we might need a decoy or something. I didn't tell you because I thought you would think it was stupid, but I guess it was pretty smart because now he has my 'I survived Atlantis' coin and we have what seems to be the magic coin."

"Okay," Sam said. "You were very cool Trip. Way to go. Now lets get going before Captain Pickle Breath comes back."

"Why do you keep calling him that?" Emily said as they began to move toward the doorway where they'd seen the stranger disappear.

"He smells horrible and I hate pickles," Sam said. "Besides, what do you think we should call him?"

"I don't know," Emily said. "I kind of hoped we wouldn't need to call him anything because I kind of hoped we wouldn't see him again."

Trip stopped and turned around to look at Emily. "You've got to be kidding," he said incredulously. "This is just getting good."

"I was afraid of that," Emily said.

"You're free to go home if you want, Emily," Trip said a little more sympathetically. "I wouldn't think you were chicken."

"No. You're right," she said with more resolve than she felt. "We can't quit now."

"What about you Sam?" Trip asked as he looked at his best friend.

"I'm in!" he answered enthusiastically.

"Alright then," Trip said as he pointed toward the door. "After Pickle Breath!"

Trip put his hand on his stomach and puffed out a sigh. He'd never had butterflies in his stomach quite like this before, but he'd also never been quite this excited. The three friends moved through the dark tunnel by feeling their way along the rough stone wall. After just a few minutes, Trip, who was in front, stopped abruptly, fell forward and let out a grunt. Emily and Sam almost fell on top of him but both kept their balance.

"You okay, Trip?" Emily whispered. She was afraid Pickle Breath might appear at any moment.

"Yeah. I probably bruised my shin, but I also think I found the way out. There are some stairs here."

They climbed the stairs as quietly as possible, stopping every minute or so to listen for the stranger. The higher they climbed, the more light began to pour down the winding stone staircase. They could hear noises from outside and knew they were going to exit the tunnel outside the giant mansion.

The exit was a small cave-like opening obscured by bushes and vines. When Trip was close enough to the entrance to see outside, he turned and put his hand up behind him to stop his friends.

"What?" Sam whispered loudly.

Trip put his finger up to his lips signaling for them to be as quiet as possible. Then he made a downward motion signaling for them to crouch down low. "I see him," Trip said as quietly as he could. "He's by the well opening my backpack." He pointed to a little clearing behind some thick wisteria vines. "Let's move over there. This is right where he'll come when he finds my Atlantis coin."

Trip, Sam and Emily moved as quickly and as quietly as possible to the spot Trip had indicated. All three dropped to their bellies and found small openings in the vines where they could see through to the well. Emily held her breath most of the time and just breathed in and out when she had to. Trip tried to relax and ignore an itch he had on his nose. And Sam tried not to panic as sweat steadily dripped off the end of his chin.

After about three minutes, which seemed more

like three hours to Emily and the boys, the strange bearded man let out an angry howl. He threw the coin, which landed within five feet of where the children hid, noisily made his way toward the staircase they had left moments earlier and disappeared in the passageway below.

Trip, Emily and Sam didn't move a muscle.

CHAPTER
12

Time Will Fly

When he was sure Pickle Breath was gone, Trip let out a sigh and scratched his nose. He looked at his friends. Sam and Emily were both a little pale. In fact, Trip thought Emily's lips and the rest of her face were now the same color – white as a sheet. "Whew, that was close," he said with a nervous chuckle.

"Yeah," Sam added weakly.

Emily just nodded.

Trip looked at his watch. "It is almost one o'clock. Didn't he say something was important about the 13th hour?"

"That's right," Sam said. The color was beginning to return to his cheeks. "In military and nautical time, the 13th hour is one o'clock."

"What do you think, Emily?" Trip asked. He was trying to help her get her mind off the strange man.

"Uh, right," she stammered. "The 13th hour."

"Emily, are you okay?" Sam asked. He had just

noticed how pale she had become.

"I'm okay," she said. "Just a little nauseous or something, but I'm getting over it."

Satisfied, Trip said, "Let's go have a look at the well before Old Man Pickle Breath comes back."

As they walked through the brush to the side of the stone well, Trip removed the real coin from his pocket. When they reached the well, Sam began to brush dirt and leaves from the stone around the top.

"There it is!" Emily exclaimed.

"There's what?" Trip asked.

"There's the message, Trip!" Sam said with a little disgust in his voice. "Don't you remember the message?"

"I remember," said Trip defensively.

Trip pulled the crumpled computer print-out from his pocket and looked at the notes they had scribbled down when they had been in the library. He read out loud, "To set it free you must let go. Time will fly, away you'll go." Emily traced her finger over the words carved in the stone around the top of the well.

"Yep, that's definitely what it says," she said. "What next, guys? I don't think we want to be here when Pickle Breath comes back."

Trip looked at his watch again. "We have to try

something," he said matter-of-factly. "It is almost one o'clock. We should hear that bell over at the church any minute."

"What do you think we're supposed to do?" Sam asked.

"That's the problem," Trip said. "I'm not sure."

"Well, it seems kind of obvious to me," Emily said. Both boys looked at her. "The truth is in water, right?"

"Right," Trip said as he and Sam both nodded their heads.

"Well," Emily continued, "there is water in the well. Pickle Breath said the 13 on the coin was for the 13th hour and the well itself says you have to 'let it go' to set time free. Don't you think that means we have to drop the coin in the water that's in the well?"

"Maybe so," Sam said excitedly.

Trip was a little more reluctant. "But then the coin will be gone, Emily. Do you know how deep that thing is? What if you're wrong?"

"It's possible," she said, "but not likely." She said the last part with a sly grin on her face.

"Sh-h-h," Sam said holding his finger to his lips. "Listen." He paused for a few seconds and then said, "I think I hear him."

As the three friends stopped talking to listen, they

did hear old Pickle Breath, and boy was he angry. He was yelling something. They couldn't make out every word, but Trip was sure he was saying something about "they're no different" and "you nosy kids" and "hanging". "We've got to do something. He's almost here," Sam urged.

At that moment the church bell tower started playing the simple melody that always preceded the chiming of the hour. "Put your hands on the well," Emily insisted. The man had reached the mouth of the tunnel and had advanced into a dead run toward the children. He was waving the club-like torch above his head and yelling.

"You have to drop the coin in the well, Trip!" Emily implored him.

The tune at the Church had ended and the big bell would strike one in a matter of seconds. The stranger was so close that he was almost within striking distance with his flaming torch. Trip wavered. He was afraid to let go of the coin and stood frozen in fear.

"Let go of the coin, Trip!" Sam yelled. The fear in his voice was unmistakable.

It all seemed like it happened in slow motion to Trip. Somehow he managed to uncurl his sweaty fingers that had been gripping the coin. He felt it slip away from his hand and he leaned over the well to watch it turn over

and over in the air as it fell. Sam and Emily gripped the well and closed their eyes in preparation for whatever was to come, whether it be something magic, or just a blow from the torch.

The clock struck one as the coin's splash echoed in the cavern of the well. At that moment, some sort of creature – something like a giant and fierce-looking hawk – emerged from the well and swooped straight toward Pickle Breath. The old man stopped dead in his tracks, dropped his torch in the dirt, fell to the ground and protected his head with his arms. The bird circled back around. It's wings made such a strong wind that Trip, Emily and Sam had to hang on to the wall of the well to keep from being swept off their feet. "Hang on tight!" Trip yelled. It was difficult to hear him because of the loud flapping of the wings.

All of a sudden, the Hawk's talons opened and came toward the children. Sam and Emily screamed, and Trip couldn't make any noise at all. He gritted his teeth and waited for the sharp talons to dig into his skin. But instead of grabbing the children, the hawk took hold of the bar that normally holds a pulley to raise and lower a bucket into the well. Then, the whole well just seemed to lift right out of the ground. But it wasn't violent or destructive like Trip thought it should be. It lifted out of the ground like it was meant to do it. The bird lifted the well just a foot or two at first and paused, like it was waiting for something.

"Maybe we're supposed to climb on," Emily said. All three of them had let go of the well when it had started to rise. She only hesitated a few seconds, then she shimmied up onto the wall of the well. "I'm finished being scared," she announced. "Let's go, guys."

The two boys looked at each other and then back at Pickle Breath who had just looked up from where he'd been hiding his head under his arms and was starting to get up. "Let's go," Sam said as he pushed Trip toward the well that was impossibly being held a foot off the ground by an impossibly large winged creature.

"Okay," he said. They quickly climbed onto the wall of the well. Immediately, the bird began to rise higher. He once again flew right over Pickle Breath, but this time holding the stone well that passed just above the old man's head. As they climbed higher and higher, the old Miller Place and the town of Mount Pleasant grew smaller and smaller and then disappeared altogether as they flew into a fluffy white cloud.

CHAPTER

13

The Fall

"Wahoo!" Sam hollered. "This is awesome!"

"This is crazy!" Trip exclaimed. He had a dumbfounded grin on his face and his knuckles were white from hanging on to the well so tightly.

"This can't be real," Emily added. "I must be dreaming."

The three friends were soaring through the clouds with the wind blowing in their faces and through their hair. They were riding on a stone well that was being carried by a giant hawk.

"I wouldn't believe it was true if it weren't happening to me," Sam said.

They flew along in silence except for the flapping of the giant bird's wings. Finally, Trip voiced what they were all thinking. "Where do you think we're going?"

"I was wondering the same thing," Emily said. "But it seems like the bird knows where it's going," she said as she pointed toward the hawk. At that moment, the bird stopped flapping its wings, started to glide and began to dip its head.

"I have a bad feeling about this," Sam said.

"Yeah," Trip answered. "Hang on, guys!"

The hawk entered into a full dive through the cloud. The well swung up behind the bird while Trip, Sam and Emily clung to it with all their might as they screamed at the top of their lungs.

It was Trip who lost his grip first. Sam saw Trip's fingers slip, one by one, off of the metal bar the hawk was gripping with his talons. He lunged to catch his friend and grabbed Trip's wrist with one hand while hanging onto the well with his other hand. The force of the hawk's steep dive and the weight of his friend was more than Sam could handle. As his hand slipped off the bar, he grabbed Emily's ankle. He looked at her with eyes that were pleading for help. In her eyes all he could see was utter terror. The hawk jerked downward into a steeper dive, and Emily's hands, too, slipped off the well. In a colorful flash of light, the well disappeared as Trip, Emily and Sam fell through the clouds flailing their arms and legs and screaming louder than they'd ever screamed before.

The giant hawk stopped its dive and swooped upward into a loop in the air. Its wings were spread wide as it descended gracefully in the downward part of the loop and came underneath the children. Trip, Sam and then Emily each fell safely onto the feathery back of the giant hawk. All three pressed their bodies as flat and as close to the bird's feathers as they possibly could and wept loudly. After several minutes, Emily looked over at Sam and Trip and her sobs began to turn to laughter. The boys looked up at her, and they too began to laugh.

"We're saved!" she screamed in relief. "I can't believe it!"

"I thought we were goners," Sam said.

"You made it quite difficult to discard the well. Because you wouldn't let go is why you fell," they heard an unfamiliar voice say.

"Who said that?" Trip said.

"Well, I did, of course. Did you think it was a horse?" the voice said.

Trip looked toward the bird's head, but still saw no one but Emily and Sam on the back of the hawk.

"Who is 'I'?" Trip asked.

"Why do you ask from whom you've heard? Do you not know it is I, the bird?" the voice said. Trip saw the bird's beak move as he heard the voice speak.

"The hawk talks!" Trip exclaimed.

"Yeah, I saw it too," Emily said.

60

Sam just stared.

"Of course I talk, I talk every day. And I have important things to say," the bird answered.

Trip didn't know what to say. He was still in shock from their traumatic fall and was now even more surprised to find himself on the back of a giant talking hawk.

The hawk continued. "I've been expecting you to come my way since I saw you find the coin by the fence Thursday."

"Where are you taking us?" Emily asked.

"A different time and place you must go to help the children from long ago. A difficult riddle you must help them discover, and complete the lost treasure that Digger uncovered."

"What children, what riddle?" Trip asked.

"For now that is all that my beak will say, I'll have more to say another day."

For the rest of the flight, Trip, Emily and Sam asked the bird questions and tried to get him to speak again, but the hawk did not utter another word. By the time they broke through the clouds, Trip was beginning to wonder if he had imagined the whole conversation.

The hawk gracefully soared toward the earth and glided along just above the treetops. The children saw the ocean, a beach and sand dunes. Woods thick with oak, pine and palmetto trees stopped abruptly at the edge of the dunes, which sloped toward a beach that ran into gentle, foaming waves. The children were close enough to hear the waves roll in toward the beach.

"This looks kind of like around home," Trip said.

"Yeah, but no houses or anything," Emily said.

Sam slapped his arm and then held up his fingers to display a mosquito carcass. "Feels like home too," he said. "Same giant, bloodthirsty mosquitoes. But that one was really huge!"

The hawk swooped down and landed smoothly on the beach. He dipped his left wing and the children slid down to the sandy surface. As soon as they had their feet on the ground, the bird began to flap his wings and lift off the beach. Trip, Sam and Emily shielded their eyes from the sand the flapping stirred. As soon as the bird lifted off, Trip ran down the beach yelling after the bird, "Hey! Where are you going? Come back here!"

Sam and Emily followed closely behind. Sam picked up a stick and threw it toward the giant hawk. "Don't leave us!" he screamed.

CHAPTER
14

Big Problems

The children squinted hard as they shielded their eyes from the sun. They were trying to keep the giant hawk in sight. As the bird disappeared over the horizon, Trip turned toward his friends. "Now what?" he said. "We don't even have my backpack anymore."

"Or the coin," Emily added.

"We can't freak out, guys," Sam said. "We have to think."

"My dad always says that it is important not to panic in an emergency," Trip added.

"Well, I would definitely say this qualifies as an emergency," Emily said.

The three friends laughed nervously.

"Okay, let's see what we can find," Trip said.

Trip, Emily and Sam turned toward the woods and walked through the dunes away from the surf rolling in behind them.

"It would be great if I had on two shoes," Sam

63

said as they walked along.

Trip and Emily laughed.

"Yeah, Sam, I've been wondering what happened to your shoe," Emily said.

"Uh, I lost it when we were trying to rescue you," Sam said.

"Oh, sorry," she said. "But, thanks."

"You're welcome," Sam said with a sheepish grin.

The three friends were so engrossed in their conversation and looking at Sam's shoeless foot as they walked that they did not immediately notice the size of the trees as they approached the woods. It was Emily who noticed it first. She suddenly stopped walking and stared in front of her. The boys took another few steps and then turned around to look at her.

"What Emily?" Trip said.

"Look at that palm tree," she said pointing to a tree not far from where they were standing. "It is gigantic!"

"Whoa," Sam said. "You're right."

Trip was slowly turning in a circle, surveying their surroundings. Trip's jaw dropped as he watched a ghost crab scurry to its hole. The crab was as big as a cat and the hole was equally big. "Did you see that?" he asked.

About that time, a giant seagull that was at least as

big as one of the kindergartners at Trip's school squawked loudly as it circled overhead. Emily screamed.

"It's huge!" Sam exclaimed.

"Come on, let's get off the beach," Trip said. All three broke into a full run towards the giant trees. As they reached the edge of the woods, Sam spotted an opening at the bottom of a tremendous live oak tree. "In there," he said as he pointed toward the opening in the tree.

The children ducked into the hollow space at the base of the tree and sat cross-legged on the ground.

"This can't be real," Emily said.

"Maybe not," Trip answered. "But it sure feels real, so we need to figure out what to do."

"You're right," she said, feeling a little bit scolded.

"The hawk wanted us to get on the well, right?" Sam said.

"That is what it seemed like," Trip said. "It didn't want Pickle Breath, though."

"Yeah," Emily added. "It seemed like the hawk had the whole thing planned out – like there was something it wanted us to do. It was trying to tell us something, but it was hard to understand. You know, like the weird way it was talking and all."

"Why is everything so big here?" Sam asked,

changing the subject.

"Maybe we're just small," Emily said.

"I don't know," he answered. "But the whole thing is really weird."

"The hawk said something about a riddle and Digger, right?" Trip changed the subject back to the bird. "Emily, you can always remember the poems we read at school. Do you remember what the hawk said?"

"Well, I know it said that it was expecting us since Thursday when you and Sam found the coin. But it seemed like the most important thing it said went something like, 'A different time and place you must go to help the people from long ago. A difficult riddle you must help them discover, and find the lost treasure that Digger uncovered.'"

"Wow, that's amazing, Emily! I think that's right," Sam said.

"Yeah, really close," Trip answered. "But I know there was something about children. Maybe it was 'help the *children* from long ago'," he said.

"Yeah, you're right. That was it," Emily said. "We should write that down."

Trip reached for his pocket to get the map they'd printed out at the library so he could write down their clue, but before he had a chance to remember that he didn't have a pen or a pencil to write with, something else grabbed his attention. As his hand slid into his pocket, his fingers hit something cool and hard. He wrapped his hand around the object and pulled it out of his pocket.

CHAPTER
15
Hula Dog

"What is . . .?" Trip's voice trailed off. Sam and Emily looked at him questioningly. "You saw me drop the coin in the well, right?" he asked his friends.

"Right. So?" Sam asked.

Trip held his hand out in front of Sam and Emily and uncurled his fingers. "So, look what I found in my pocket!" he said. All three stared at the object in Trip's hand. There sitting flat on his outstretched palm, was what looked like their coin. It had the same flying "13" and the same Latin words, but it seemed shinier, almost like it was glowing.

"Is it our same coin?" Sam asked. He reached over and took the coin out of Trip's hand. He turned it over and looked at the other side. There he saw the familiar image of water surrounded by a chain and a lock. "What?" he exclaimed. "How'd it get in your pocket?"

"I don't know," Trip answered. "But there is one thing I know. Nothing around here makes any sense."

Trip looked at Emily and saw that she was deep in thought. "What are you thinking, Emily?" he asked.

"I was just thinking that, at first, I thought we had traveled to another time in the past – you know, time travel, like in that movie we saw at school. But now, I don't know. If that's it, why is everything so gigantic? Maybe we're in a different kind of place. Like a different world."

"Or, maybe *we're* just different," Sam said cocking his head to one side as he shrugged his shoulders. "You know, because of the magic coin."

Emily looked at Sam and nodded her head in approval of Sam's idea. "Good thought, Sam."

Trip joined in. "It is true that except for the things that have happened because of the coin, like the well flying and the talking bird, everything else looks pretty familiar – just really big!"

Trip picked up a twig in the dirt near where he sat in the hollow space under the tree. He made a loud sound in his throat and spit on the ground. He then began to stir the spit and dirt together.

"Gross, Trip!" Emily exclaimed. "What are you doing?"

Sam laughed and smiled approvingly.

"I'm making mud. Then I'm going to dip this twig

in the mud and try to write down the clue you remembered on our map."

"Oh, that might work," she said, now sounding more impressed than grossed-out.

"It's not my lucky blue pencil," he said, "But I think it will work. We did this one time as part of a scout achievement during a camping trip." Slowly, Trip began to scratch an abbreviated version of the message in mud onto the paper. With help from Emily and Sam, Trip painstakingly wrote out the words:

1. *Different time place*
2. *Help kids from long ago*
3. *Riddle discover, find lost treasure*
4. *Digger*

It was a little hard to read, but better than nothing.

"Well, we're not going to help any kids find a treasure if we're hiding under this oak tree," Sam said. "Let's get going."

Trip silently prayed to God for help and then said, "Okay, I'm ready." Just as they were about to move from the hiding place, they began to hear loud crashing and crunching of sticks and leaves as if something large was walking through the woods. As the sound got louder and louder, the three looked at each other with glances that said, "Don't move!"

A shadow fell over the entrance to their hiding place. Trip, who was sitting closest to the opening, carefully repositioned himself so that he could try to see what was making all that noise. What he saw nearly made his heart stop. There before him were two giant men, and one of them looked just like Pickle Breath – only a lot bigger! "What's he doing here?" Trip thought. The other man was even bigger and stronger looking than Pickle Breath. He had on loose-fitting tattered pants, old black boots and a tight, sleeveless shirt. On his bulging bicep was a tattoo of a scruffy looking dog that looked like it was dancing and wearing a hula skirt.

"They're not going to get away this time," Pickle Breath was saying. "I don't care if they are mere babes. The coin they have should belong to me! All of Digger's treasure will belong to me."

"We don't have to hurt 'em, Captain. Both of them is little." Hula Dog said in a deep voice. "We can try to scare it out of 'em first."

As the men moved on through the woods and away from the hiding spot, Trip, Sam and Emily let out a collective sigh of relief.

"Did you see who it was?" Trip whispered.

"I heard," Emily answered as Sam nodded his head.

71

"How can he be here? Didn't we leave him behind?"

"I don't know, but did you see how big he and that other guy were? They were huge!" Trip said.

"Do you think they were talking about us?" Sam asked.

"Maybe, but Hula Dog acted like he had seen whoever they were talking about and he said 'both' of them," Trip observed. "There are three of us."

"Who is Hula Dog?" Emily asked.

"Oh, the other guy had a weird tattoo on his arm that looked like a dog doing the hula," Trip explained.

Sam laughed and said, "Well, he should be easy to recognize then."

Trip smiled and said, "Yeah, I guess."

Emily chimed in, "If they are talking about the kids that the hawk said we're supposed to help, we need to get moving."

"Right," Trip said. "We've got to find those other kids before Pickle Breath and Hula Dog get to them. I have a feeling we may be their only hope."

"Who do you think they are?" Sam asked.

"I don't know, but I guess we can find out when we find them."

Emily had already pushed past the boys and out into the open. "Guys, please," she said as she looked back toward the tree. "Less talkin', more walkin'."

Sam and Trip looked at each other and laughed. They moved out from under the tree and Sam said with a smile in his voice, "Well, which way boss?"

She smiled and then said, "I guess we should follow the trail Pickle Breath and Hula Dog made for now, and then see what happens."

Trip and Sam nodded in agreement and feeling more important, and less frightened, they began moving in the same direction the giant men had gone.

CHAPTER
16
The Argument

As hard as Trip, Emily and Sam tried to keep up, the distance between them and the two giant men steadily increased until the children had lost sight of them completely. "I'm so thirsty," Sam complained. "Can't we stop and rest?" Trip and Emily looked at each other and rolled their eyes. When nobody answered him, Sam added, "What? You're not tired? Where are we going anyway? Do you even know what we're looking for?" He paused for a minute and then added, "I'm just wondering what we're doing here."

Trip let out an exasperated sigh, stopped walking and turned to look at Sam. "Sam, buddy, please. I don't know, okay, I don't know about anything. Can you understand that? I – DON'T – KNOW!"

"Trip, calm down. Sam does have a point," Emily added.

"I do?" said Sam, surprised and pleased that Emily had seemingly jumped in on his side.

"Well, now that Pickle Breath and Hula Dog are out of sight, we really don't have a plan," Emily said. "I'm pretty tired too. Maybe we should stop and think."

"Well you're going to have to forget about that, Emily," Trip shot back, clearly annoyed. "You should've thought about what was going to happen."

"What do you mean?" Emily asked.

"Well, you're the one who got us into this to start with," he answered.

"Are you kidding me?" Emily asked with disbelief in her voice. "You're the one who found that stupid coin and then dragged me into it."

"Yeah, but who's idea was it to jump onto a flying well? 'I'm done being scared, come on guys'," Trip mocked.

Tears were beginning to well up in Emily's eyes. Sam, who was feeling a little bit guilty for starting the argument, yelled, "Trip, don't be a jerk. We have all been in this from the beginning."

"Fine! I'm just saying that whining is not going to help anything," Trip said.

"I'm not whining," Sam said, offended at Trip's accusation. "I just think we need to make a better plan."

As the boys continued to argue, they got louder and louder. Emily tried to interrupt them, but they were so engrossed in their argument, they didn't even hear her. Finally she put a hand on each of their shoulders and yelled as loud as she could, "STOP!"

Surprised at her outburst, the boys both turned to look at her, stopped arguing for just a few seconds, then simultaneously began to tell her why the other was at fault.

"I don't care!" Emily yelled again. With both boys staring at her, she said a little more calmly, "Can't you see we're falling apart? If we're going to survive this, we've got to stick together!"

"The young lady has a point," a deep voice said.

Emily, Sam and Trip spun around, and to their horror saw Hula Dog standing a short distance away behind some bushes, Trip screamed and yelled, "It's Hula Dog! Run!"

Hula Dog laughed and said, "You think I can't catch you?"

Hula Dog's comment made Trip's blood run cold and lit a fire under all three kids. They turned in the opposite direction and ran with all their might. They crashed through the underbrush, desperate to get away. Suddenly, Sam went sprawling as he tripped over a root. He scrambled to his feet and continued to run. But before he could catch up to his friends, a giant hand grabbed him. Sam shut his eyes tight when he felt his feet leave the ground. When he opened his eyes, he was face to face with the man they called "Hula Dog".

"Well, now," the man was saying. "I don't believe we've met."

Sam could not answer. He couldn't move. He was paralyzed with fear.

When Trip and Emily saw that Sam had been captured, they stopped running. "Hula has Sam," Trip said. He was breathing heavily from running so hard. "What should we do?" Emily asked. She was leaning over with her hands on her knees. She was also trying to catch her breath. "I think we have to go back," Trip said reluctantly. "We can't risk letting Hula Dog take him. You were right," he said, putting his hand on her shoulder. "We have to stick together."

As they back-tracked toward Sam, Trip felt his stomach tighten in fear. He reached out for Emily's hand. Her hand was cold and clammy and he knew she was just as scared as he was. When they got close enough to easily be heard, Trip called out with more conviction than he felt, "Hey, let him go!"

Hula dog lowered Sam closer to the ground and looked at Trip and Emily. His face lit up with a big toothy grin, and in what seemed like an almost friendly voice, he

said, "Greetings, sojourners. Little Ben and Susan Miller have been expecting you for quite some time. What took you so long?"

CHAPTER
17
Good or Bad?

Sam stopped kicking his legs and looked up at the huge man they were calling Hula Dog. "You've got the wrong kids, mister," he said. "Just put me down and let me go."

"Yeah," Trip added. "We don't know what you're talking about. We don't know Ben and Susan Miller."

Emily started to say, "Maybe they're the kids that found . . .", but she was interrupted by Trip who gave her a pointed look that said he thought she should keep her ideas quiet for the moment. "As I was saying," Trip said. "We don't know a Ben or a Susan except for Ben Walker on my soccer team, and well, he obviously doesn't live here."

"No, you don't know them," Hula Dog agreed. "But as keeper of the 13th magic coin of Digger's treasure, you have been appointed to help them complete the task they started."

When Trip opened his mouth to speak, his voice

came out much higher and nervous-sounding than he intended. "You're crazy. We don't have it," he lied. "I don't even know what you're talking about."

Hula Dog laughed heartily. Trip and Emily cringed as they saw Sam shake up and down with every ripple of laughter. The large man whistled through his teeth and then said, "Let's see what Fowler has to say about that." In the distance, the children heard the now familiar flapping sound of giant hawk wings. As the flapping sound got louder and louder, Trip found himself more and more confused. He had thought the bird to be friendly toward them. He had even thought the bird was supposed to be their guide in this strange mystery. "Maybe this was a different bird," he thought to himself. Finally, the bird came into view and then swooped down to land next to Hula Dog. Trip recognized it immediately as the bird that had delivered them to the beach.

"Hello, Fowler, great bird of the sky," Hula Dog was saying.

The bird answered, "Hello, my friend, brave and strong. With these three here, it won't be long."

"They say they do not have the magic coin, Fowler. What do you say?"

"I say that argument is weak. The coin in the well set me free to speak. Once the magic was set in motion,

81

the coin returned with a magic potion."

Upon hearing the part about the magic potion, Trip reached into his pocket and pulled out the coin. Before he realized what he was doing, he said, "What magic potion? It looks pretty much the same to me."

Still in Hula Dog's grasp, Sam let his head fall forward and in a voice that sounded like part sigh and part groan, he said, "Trip, No!" Emily also yelled his name and grabbed his arm, but it was too late. Trip felt his face get hot as he realized that the coin, their only bargaining chip, lay exposed in his hand right in front of their giant enemy. In desperation, he clamped his hand around the coin and screamed at the bird. "You tricked me! Whose side are you on anyway? I thought you were one of the good guys . . . uh, birds . . . oh, whatever. You know what I mean! Why are you helping him?" he said motioning to Hula Dog.

"Trick you I did not do," Fowler, the hawk, answered. "You speak of sides. We side with you."

"Trip, don't believe him!" Sam said as he struggled against Hula Dog's grasp. "If they are on our side, then why am I still stuck in his sweaty hands?"

Emily added, "Yeah, and what about him being with Pickle Breath and talking about getting those kids."

"If his intentions were to bring you destruction,

you would no longer be here to seek your instruction," the Hawk said.

Hula Dog lowered Sam to the ground and released his grasp. Sam quickly ran to his friends and moved around behind them. His clothes were wet with sweat. It was a mixture of Hula Dog's sweat and his own.

Hula Dog began to speak. "Ben and Susan Miller came from your time a few weeks ago. Captain Bartholomew heard about their arrival and discovered that they held a piece of Digger's treasure, the coin with the flying 13. He was crazy with rage and envy. So I vowed to secretly help protect Ben and Susan from his wrath. He still seeks the Millers and their coin."

"But I have the coin," Trip said. "And who is Captain Bartholomew?"

"The Captain is the man you saw with me in the woods," Hula Dog said.

"Pickle Breath?" Emily said. "But he knows we have the coin."

"Ah, this I believe I can solve in part. The time now precedes the time he did depart," Fowler said.

"So, he hasn't actually traveled into the future yet." Trip stated thoughtfully.

"Well, why is he so huge here?" Sam asked. By now he had almost recovered from his previous ordeal.

"He was normal size in our time."

"The change is not in him, but in you. Journey to past centuries shrunk the Millers too." Fowler said. "Going forward must not have that effect, when you return home your size may correct."

"Okay, Hula Dog," Emily said. "What if we do believe you? What next?"

Hula laughed and said, "Is that what you call me? Hula Dog? An appropriate name," he said as he flexed his bicep with the strange tattoo. "I am called Grimsley, but you may call me what you wish."

"All right, Grimsley," Trip said. "How do we find Ben and Susan?"

"Fowler here can take you to them."

"Then what?" Emily asked. "What are we supposed to do?"

"I don't know," he stated matter-of-factly.

"You don't know?" Sam asked.

"With Ben and Susan you will have to discover, we know not what you are to uncover," Fowler said.

Sam, Emily and Trip all turned toward each other and made a tight huddle as they quickly discussed what they'd just learned. After a minute or two, Trip turned to Grimsley and said, "Okay. We've all agreed. We'll at least go meet the Millers."

CHAPTER
18

The Hideout

Trip, Sam and Emily clung tightly to the feathers on Fowler's enormous back as the hawk flapped his wings to rise above the trees. Trip looked at his friends. Both appeared tense but had determined looks on their faces. He noticed that his own teeth were clinched tightly together, and he imagined that he looked much the same way as Sam and Emily. He had given up trying to explain in his mind the things that had happened since he first dropped the coin in the well at the Miller place. Now he was just trying to understand what he was supposed to do.

Sam interrupted Trip's thoughts by saying, "Things don't really look that strange from up here."

"Yeah," Emily added. "I was just thinking maybe it was all a dream." She reached over to Sam and pinched his toe on the foot where he'd lost his shoe earlier.

"Ouch!" Sam said with a befuddled look on his face. "What'd you do that for?"

Emily laughed. "Just checking. Guess it's not a dream."

"You're just now figuring that out?" Trip said with a grin. He was rubbing a long scratch that he had gotten on his arm from a sharp branch when they were running from Grimsley.

Emily smiled back at him and said, "No. I was just hoping. Of course, we are sitting on the back of a giant talking hawk." She paused for a moment and then said, "Sorry about before, Trip."

"Yeah, me too," he answered.

Sam peered over Fowler's giant wing. "Hey, we're over the ocean. Where are we going?"

Fowler, who had been quiet up to this point, cleared his throat and said, "Ben and Susan are hidden away, across the water they've spent their days. Bartholomew does seek the pair, their lives he does not intend to spare."

Emily shuttered. "You mean he wants to kill them?" she asked.

"If that is what it takes, he will. His angry greed he must fulfill."

As he spoke, Fowler began his descent toward a small island across a wide section of water from where they had been moments earlier. They flew over some stones that looked like they had been placed there in an orderly manner. Some of the stones had been laid to form what was beginning to look like a low round wall. It reminded Trip of the well they had left behind somewhere between home and this strange new world they now inhabited. Fowler glided over the stones and flew low along the shoreline for what seemed like a long way. Finally, he lowered his talons and gently landed on the sandy surface. Like before, he lowered his left wing and the three children slid to the ground.

"Now what, Fowler?" Trip asked.

In response, Fowler made an unusual screeching sound, flapped his wings and flew away.

Trip, Emily and Sam looked at each other. Emily shrugged her shoulders and said, "Whatever."

Trip turned and started walking toward the underbrush that ran up to the edge of the beach. "Come on," he said as he sighed with frustration. Sam and Emily turned to follow him. They were on a narrow stretch of beach that had several large branches that appeared to be coming out of the sand. They were bleached almost white and formed complex and tangled-looking formations with their leafless and smooth branches. To the miniature-sized children, the formations looked tremendous. Green pieces of seaweed were draped over some of the lower branches that must have been exposed to the ocean water when the tide came up really high, like happens on a full moon.

As they made their way past the branches, Emily stopped abruptly. "Did you hear that?" she asked the boys.

"No, what?" Trip answered. Sam was shaking his head, indicating that he hadn't heard it either.

"Sh-h-h. Quiet," she said. She strained to listen.

"Hey, over here," they heard someone whisper in a hoarse voice.

The three looked toward one of the most complex looking branch formations.

"Ben, is that you?" Trip said peering in the direction of the voice. He still didn't see anyone.

"Yeah. Over here." Ben was hiding behind some of the seaweed covered branches. He had stuck his arm out and waved it at Trip, Sam and Emily. "Hurry," he said. "Bartholomew has spies."

Trip and his friends cautiously approached the hideout. A boy that seemed to be about 11 years old stood there pulling aside a long piece of seaweed. He looked dirty and tired. His hair was stiff and disheveled like hair that dried in the sun with salt water still in it. His face was pink with sunburn and he had a huge grin on his face. Because he was small, like they were, Trip was confident that this was the boy they were looking for.

"Come on in," the boy said. "Man, am I glad to see you! Fowler told us you were coming. My name is Ben, and this is my sister, Susan," he said motioning to a younger girl sitting in a wide hole that had been dug in the sand in their makeshift fort. She smiled shyly at them and said, "Hi."

Trip introduced himself, Sam and Emily and then looked around the fort. It looked like the Millers had been spending a lot of time there. There were blankets crumpled in the corner, the remains of chicken bones and a large bucket full of water. Several games of tick-tack-toe and hangman had been scratched into the sand alongside the large hole.

"What are you doing in here?" Sam said. "Don't you guys have a mystery to solve?"

"Yeah, come on," Trip said. "Quit playing games. Let's go."

"Hold on, we can't," Ben said forcefully. "We'll have to wait until night. We can't risk being seen." Trip looked at the fear in Ben's eyes and decided he should listen to the boy's advice. "Besides, we have a lot to fill you in on," Ben said.

Chapter
19
The Journal

Relieved to finally start getting answers, Trip motioned to Sam and Emily, and they all quickly ducked under the branches into the driftwood fort. When they stepped down into the crudely dug hole in the sand, Trip realized how deep the hole actually was. The sand ledge around him was up to the level of his rib cage.

"Wow, this is deep," Emily was saying. "This must've taken you forever to build."

Susan Miller looked small and vulnerable leaning against the sandy wall of their fort. She held her knees tightly to her chest and rested her cheeks on her knees so that her eyes barely peered out. Emily wasn't sure what else to say to the girl so she simply said, "Hi" and then sat down next to her. Susan glanced at her and then quickly looked away.

Ben looked at Susan and then Emily. Apologetically he said, "We've been under a lot of stress."

Then, changing gears, he said, "We dug our hideout

deep enough so that we could pull those branches and driftwood over the top and be completely out of sight." He pointed to a small pile of sticks and driftwood a few feet away. "So far, we've done that every night while we take turns sleeping."

"Man," Sam said in disbelief. "That's unbelievable!"

"Yeah, wow," Trip added. "What I'm wondering is how in the world we're supposed to help you."

Emily stood up again and said, "Fowler said something about helping you find Digger's lost treasure. What do you know about that?"

"I know a little," Ben said. "But first everybody needs to sit down so we don't give away where we're hiding."

Ben, Emily, Sam and Trip all crouched down in the hole to sit down around Susan. Each of them had just enough room to lean against the sandy wall, but with all of them in there together, the hole seemed way too small.

"What happened to your shoe, man?" Ben said pointing at Sam's shoeless foot. "Oh, I lost it under the steps of your house when a rotten board broke," Sam answered.

Ben nodded as they all wiggled into their places. Emily found herself touching shoulders with Susan who was still trying very hard to keep to herself.

Emily tilted her head toward Susan and whispered, "Susan, are you okay?" Susan nodded her head slightly and whispered back, "I'm just scared, and I want to go home."

Emily wiggled her arm free and put it around Susan's shoulders. She gave her a slight squeeze and said, "Yeah, me too. But we have to be brave so we *can* get back home. Together I think we will do it. We have to believe we can."

For the first time, Susan lifted her head from her knees, looked at Emily and gave her the slightest of smiles. Emily grinned and squeezed Susan's shoulder again.

Ben smiled at Emily and said, "Okay, let's get started. Here's what I know." He leaned to the side to put all his weight on his left leg and pulled a small weathered looking book from his right back pocket. It was about the size of a three-by-five photograph and had an old worn brown leather cover. A long leather string was attached to the back cover and wound several times around the small book.

"What's that?" Sam asked impatiently.

Without answering, Ben continued to unwind the long leather string from around the book. He patted the cover and said, "Susan and I found this book in a secret passage we discovered under our house in South Carolina. One day, we found the entrance near the old well on our property, and over the next few weeks began to explore it. I couldn't believe we didn't know about it before. It was really exciting. About a month after we first discovered the tunnels, Susan found a loose brick in an area of the tunnel that didn't lead anywhere. It was a dead end. We went to get some tools from our Dad's workshop, and eventually we were able to pry the loose brick out of place. What we found inside was a small wooden box containing a coin and this little book. There were also some maps, kind of like plans really, that were rolled up and slid way back in the hole."

Ben opened the book and held it up for the others to see. He showed them a page with a sketch scribbled on it.

"Hey, that's just like our coin!" Trip said.

"That's what we suspected," Ben answered. "We weren't sure how you got here, but thought it must have been the same way we did."

"On the well?" Emily asked.

Susan nodded her head while Ben answered, "Exactly. But what I don't get is how the coin got back there with you in the first place. I wonder if it is the same coin?"

"Well, do you have your coin now?" Trip asked.

"No," he answered. "Captain Bartholomew stole it from us. But Bartholomew only knows part of the riddle, so even though he stole the coin from us, he can't complete the collection."

"I guess he thought he would find the other coins in the future in the tunnels under your house in Mt. Pleasant," Emily added.

"What do you mean?" Ben asked.

"Bartholomew is the one who brought it to the future," Emily said.

Trip chimed in, "Pickle Breath, I mean Captain Bartholomew, lost the coin and we found it. We didn't know what it was for, but we accidentally made our way here anyway, I guess."

"Maybe he was able to travel with the coin just so you would have a way back to help us," Ben said. He had scrunched up his forehead and seemed to be trying hard to understand.

"I don't know," Trip answered. "But I know he didn't find what he wanted."

"The rest of the treasure?" Ben asked.

"Yeah. Pickle Breath said most of the tunnels had been filled in after you disappeared," Trip said.

"But I don't get it," Sam said. "You're from 1980

94

something, right?"

"Yeah, 1986. Aren't you?" Ben asked.

"We're from the year 2006!" Emily exclaimed.

"Huh," Ben said with surprise in his voice. "Maybe Bartholomew was sent to the wrong time because he has evil intentions."

"What do you mean?" Trip asked.

"Well, this little book is a journal recorded by one of our ancestors."

"Digger," Trip, Emily and Sam said in unison.

"Yes," Ben said. "The journal tells about a treasure of a collection of special silver coins. When complete, the coin collection would give the person who had it a rare and special power. The journal talks a lot about how a person's motives must be good and pure for the full power of the treasure to work."

"Oh," Trip said a little confused and then hesitantly added, "But I thought Digger was a pirate."

"He was when he was really young," Ben said. "But I guess something happened that made him want to help people, not hurt them."

"Maybe it had something to do with what he found out about the treasure," Emily said.

"I don't know," Ben answered. "But it seemed to be very important to him that someone find the treasure and use it for good. That's why he hid 12 of the coins, but kept the 13th coin and his journal behind the brick under his house. That way, if someone did find the treasure, they wouldn't get the power without the 13th coin. His journal says that he couldn't dig up the treasure himself because the rest of the crew that had escaped the raid when Blackbeard was killed suspected that Digger knew where it was. They would've killed him for it, but had to keep him alive in hopes that he would lead them to it one day."

"Do you know where it is?" Emily asked.

"That's what we're trying to figure out," Ben said.

"Sh-h-h-h." Everyone turned to look at Susan who was holding her finger up to her lips. "I heard something."

CHAPTER
20
Stranger in the Night

As the group quieted and listened, they didn't hear anything unusual at first. Ben looked at Susan questioningly. He was about to ask what she heard when they all heard a splashing sound followed by a squeaking noise which then repeated itself in a steady rhythm. Trip made a move toward the sticks that the Millers had gathered to pull them over the top of the hole where they were sitting. Ben grabbed Trip's wrist with a firm hand and held up his other hand with his palm facing out. He mouthed the word, "wait", and then motioned for all of them to sit low and stay quiet. Trip thought how glad he was at this moment to be so small. He wished he could be invisible too.

Ben, who had his back to the water, carefully turned around, got to his knees, pushed up on his toes and peered over the edge of the sand pit. What he saw was a man in a rowboat. He had on a suit that made him look respectable, but had removed his coat and rolled up his shirt sleeves revealing a skull and crossbones tattoo on his left forearm. "The Jolly Roger," Ben said to himself. Ben had read enough books about pirates to recognize the pirate symbol when he saw it.

Ben turned around toward the others and mouthed the word, "Pirate". Trip, who had been sitting next to Ben, lifted his head just high enough to get a glimpse of the new stranger. Not seeing the tattoo at first, Trip leaned toward Ben and in a barely audible voice said, "Are you sure?"

"Yeah, look at his arm," Ben whispered back.

The man lifted the oars as the small dinghy slid up to the beach, scraping the hull on the coarse sand. He moved to the front of the boat, put his hand on the bow and jumped onto the beach. He pulled the boat as far as he could up onto the shore and then pulled a rope from the bow toward one of the branch formations close to where the children were hiding. Trip and Ben quickly ducked down as the man tied his rope to the branches. Hearing the commotion, Sam, Emily and Susan crouched lower in the hiding spot. Emily could feel Susan trembling.

As the man moved away from them and back to the small boat, all three boys quickly and quietly lifted their heads just above the top of the sandpit so that they could see him. The man was obviously nervous and his

eyes shifted around in every direction as if he expected to be discovered at any moment. The sun was going down, and Trip thought that whatever the man was up to, he must want to be hidden by the darkness. If this place was anything like home, it would be pitch black dark in about twenty minutes.

The pirate walked toward the middle of the boat, leaned over and pulled a crude wooden box from under the seat where he had been sitting. He set it down on the seat and pulled on his coat. Ben looked at Susan excitedly and reached for her hand. "Sue, come look at this!"

Trip moved over as much as he could so that Susan could get into the spot next to her brother. Emily, who was getting tired of not being able to see what was going on, also tried to move around so she could see. In the process, she accidentally stepped on Sam's shoeless foot. Forgetting their predicament, Sam let out a high pitched, "Ow!"

The man stopped abruptly, looked in their direction, took a few steps forward, and stood there staring and listening for a full minute. As soon as Sam yelled, all the children ducked down and tried to be as still as they could be in such a confined spot. When a seagull flew overhead and squawked, the man looked at it, seemed to be satisfied that was what he'd heard and turned back toward the boat. Five tiny heads popped up once again and five sets of eyes watched the elegant looking pirate pick up the box and tuck it under his coat. Susan looked at Ben with excitement in her eyes and then back at the man. He gave the boat one last tug with his free hand, surveyed his surroundings with his suspicious, shifty eyes, picked up a large shovel from the floorboard of the dinghy and headed through the dunes toward the woods.

"What are you guys so excited about?" Emily asked. "Who was that?"

"I don't know who it was, but I have an idea," Ben answered. "There was something he had that looks awfully familiar."

"His wooden box is just like the one we found in the tunnel!" Susan added.

"The box with the book and the coin?" Sam asked.

"Right," Ben answered. "Of course it looks a lot bigger here since we're so small, but it is made the same." He opened up Digger Miller's old leather journal he'd found in the tunnel and flipped through some pages. When he found the page he was looking for he moved his finger under the written words while reading aloud, "I crafted two identical wooden boxes to hold the pieces to the treasure. The boxes are one foot wide and two inches deep, branded with the symbol of the Jolly Roger and the year 1767."

"That's the year Charles Miller built his house," Emily said.

Sam and Trip just looked at her. "How do you know that?" Sam asked.

"We read it at the library, silly. I'm good at remembering dates," she answered.

Trip pulled out their map drawn on the back of their computer print out, turned it over and read the part they had highlighted with bright yellow marker. "She's right," he said with admiration in his voice. "It also says that the place where Miller Plantation was built was 'far removed' from the town. It was secluded in an area known as Hort's Grove."

"It's hard to believe that the Miller place was considered 'far removed' from town," Sam said.

"Charles Miller had something to hide," Emily said. "Or someone to hide from."

Thinking he may already know the answer, Trip asked, "So who do you think that man was?"

Ben and Susan looked at each other and then both answered, "Digger."

CHAPTER
21

The Riddle

"If that man is Digger, then that box may be the treasure," Trip said.

"That box is not big enough for treasure!" Sam said. "Shouldn't the treasure be a big chest full of gold and stuff?"

"Not this treasure," Ben said. "As far as I can tell, this treasure has 13 unique coins and that's all."

"That's not all, Ben," Susan chimed in.

"Right. You're forgetting about the magic the coins have when they're all together," Emily added.

"I didn't forget," Ben said. "I know the coins have a special power."

"But you don't know what that power is?" Sam asked.

"Not exactly," Ben answered.

"Well, if we want to find the box, we better follow Digger," Trip said.

"I think I know where he'll hide it," Ben said.

"Susan and I have already been there two times but couldn't find anything."

Trip, Sam and Emily looked at Ben with confusion on their faces.

"There are instructions on how to find the treasure in this journal," Ben explained. "But before now we couldn't find it. Now it's starting to make sense."

"I get it," Emily said with enthusiasm. "You couldn't find it because Digger hadn't hidden it yet."

"That's what I'm thinking," Ben said.

"Well, where is he going then?" Sam asked impatiently.

Ben flipped through some of the handwritten entries and drawings in the little leather journal looking for a page he had studied many times. "Here it is," he said. "Okay, you know the old Morris Island Lighthouse in Charleston Harbor?"

The other children nodded that they did.

"Well, I think we are on Morris Island now," Ben said. "Listen to this riddle."

Ben turned his eyes toward the journal and began to read.

"To shed **LIGHT** on where the treasure is hidden, ill intentions are forbidden. Those with a Pirates' dark heart are banned, unlocked it will be by a child's innocent hand."

Ben paused and looked up at his audience who were all listening very carefully to the riddle.

Trip, who was reading over Ben's shoulder added, "The word 'light' is in all capital letters and underlined."

"Okay, go on," Sam urged.

"A stone message will mark the way, for seafaring ships and where the treasure lay. Two stones to the right and up three blocks, another loose brick will reveal my box."

"Is he talking about a lighthouse?" Trip asked.

"Susan and I think so," Ben said.

"But there's no lighthouse out here," Sam added.

"Yes, but there is one under construction," Ben answered.

Emily's eyes lit up as she remembered something. "Guys! Remember the round stone wall we saw when Fowler brought us here to Ben and Susan? I bet that's it." Ben and Susan nodded.

"Well, what are we waiting for?" Emily said. "Let's go."

CHAPTER
22
The Confrontation

Susan looked warily at the dinghy that sat pulled up on the beach where the pirate had left it only moments before. "I'm not so sure this is a good idea. I mean, that man is a pirate, and we don't really know who he is or what he might do to us if he finds us," she said.

"I don't blame you for being scared," Sam said. "Bartholomew does want to kill you."

"Sam!" Emily chided her friend. "You don't have to say everything that comes into your mind!"

"What?" Sam said. "Fowler told us that. Anyway, if he wants to kill them he'll probably want to kill us too. So we're all in the same boat."

"That's enough, Sam," Trip said. "Nobody is going to get killed."

Susan, who was looking even more frightened than before said, "So maybe we should at least wait for the pirate we think is Digger to leave."

"Fair enough," Ben said as he put a protective arm

around his little sister. "We should look over the journal some more anyway."

For the next few minutes, Ben showed the other children what Digger had recorded on the pages of his old journal. There were sketches of the 13th coin that had started their whole adventure, as well as sketches of the other twelve coins. Each was unique with markings the children did not understand.

"Do you think all these coins have something to do with time travel?" Trip wondered aloud.

"I don't know," Ben answered. "The only thing that Digger seemed sure of was that the power of the coins could only be truly harnessed by people with good intentions."

"The riddle you read earlier said something about that, didn't it?" Emily asked.

Ben nodded and then reread part of the riddle. "To shed LIGHT on where the treasure is hidden, ill intentions are forbidden. Those with a Pirates' dark heart are banned, unlocked it will be by a child's innocent hand."

"I hope there is something that will explain the riddle when we find the treasure," Sam said.

"*If* we find it," Trip added.

The children were deep in conversation when they heard the sound of someone or something crashing through the underbrush as it approached the beach. All five grew quiet and looked into the darkness to try and see what it was. In the distance, they saw the elegant pirate they thought was Digger in a full run. He no longer held the shovel, nor the box.

"He's running from something," Trip whispered. The others nodded their heads in agreement. They saw another figure burst out of the underbrush and heard the now familiar voice scream with fury. "You're a dead man Digger Miller!"

"It's Pickle Breath!" Sam exclaimed. Emily reached over and gently slapped her hand over Sam's mouth. "We need to be quiet," she whispered.

"Look at you," Bartholomew taunted Miller. "Running like a scared rat and no better than a rat!"

Digger ran past their hideout and stopped abruptly to untie his rope. When he reached his boat he put both hands on the bow and pushed with all his might. The tide had begun to recede and the dinghy, which was now further up onto the sand, budged only slightly. He dug his feet in and pushed even harder. This time the boat moved a little more, and now the entire stern rested in an inch or two of water. Bartholomew had now drawn his sword, was waving it around over his head and was nearly within spitting distance of Digger and his boat.

With one more desperate push, the boat scraped over the sand and floated into the Atlantic Ocean. Digger pushed it a few more steps, threw himself into the dinghy, picked up his oars and began to furiously row backwards away from the shore.

Bartholomew ran up to his waist in the water and tried to grab the bow of the boat, but the boat glided out of his reach. When Digger saw that he was unreachable he said, "The treasure is no good to you Capt'n. Leave it alone. This sort of treasure is worthless to a pirate."

Bartholomew, who was red-faced with rage, drew back his arm and slung his sword toward the boat as he screamed in anger. The sword stuck in the wooden seat just in front of where Digger sat. Miller laughed and said, "Not this time, Capt'n Bartholomew."

The children were so engaged with what they were watching that they didn't hear the sound of someone sneaking up behind them. They all jumped when they heard a booming voice say, "Well, look what I found Captain Bart. Prisoners."

All of the children looked up at the man in disbelief. There, looking down at them, was Grimsley.

CHAPTER
23

The Capture

"Grimsley!" Emily whispered. "What are you doing?"

Grimsley looked directly at her, shook his head "no" in a barely perceptible manner and then yelled over to Bartholomew again. "The spies were right, Captain. There's four of 'em here hiding in a hole like ferrets." Grimsley looked pointedly at Trip and then quickly shifted his eyes toward the woods.

Trip exchanged glances with the others and Ben whispered, "Go. He's giving you a chance to escape." Ben pressed the leather journal into Trip's hand.

"I won't let anything happen to you," Trip said looking at Susan. He quickly glanced at the others and said, "I'll find all of you."

As he climbed out of the hole, Trip heard Grimsley say under his breath, "Use the coin." Trip pressed his body against the warm sand and then crawled combat style for what seemed like forever. When he felt like he was far enough away, he got to his feet. While maintaining his crouched position, he ran toward the cover of the underbrush and the trees. Once there, he hid behind a small cypress tree and watched Bartholomew and Grimsley tie his friends' hands behind their backs and lead them down a path toward the same woods where he was hiding. The two men towered over the shrunken children.

Once they were in the woods, Trip followed at a safe distance. He wanted to know where Bartholomew and Grimsley were taking his friends. It wasn't long before Trip spotted a ship anchored off an area of beach on the other side of the woods. The full moon illuminated the ship just enough for Trip to see a tattered black Jolly Roger fluttering in the evening breeze. The waves were pounding the shore and a small rowboat was being guarded by two strong looking men.

As Trip hid behind the dunes, he heard the now familiar flapping of wings. He turned to see Fowler glide to the ground a few feet away from him. "Fowler, Grimsley captured Sam and Emily and the Millers! I thought he was on our side," Trip whispered in a panicky voice.

"He let you go, did he not? Your hideout was discovered, Bartholomew was hot," Fowler answered. "Now come with me to find the treasure, and deny Old Bart his one true pleasure."

"How do I know I can trust you?" Trip asked warily.

"Trust me you may or maybe you don't, but you must find the treasure to reach your homefront. Leave them now and come with me, when you have the treasure you can set them free."

Trip looked over his shoulder in the direction of the ship. His friends were being loaded into the rowboat, which he assumed would take them out to the large ship anchored off the beach. He turned back toward Fowler and approached the bird. Grabbing two fists full of feathers, Trip scrambled up onto the Bird's broad back. "I hope I'm doing the right thing," he mumbled as a new wave of fear settled in his belly.

Once they were airborne, Fowler said, "Uncertain I am of where to take you. Perhaps you can offer old Fowler a clue?"

Trip surveyed the earth below him and spotted the stones that formed the low round wall. "There!" he said pointing toward the stones. "Down there where those stones are. Ben thinks that has something to do with the treasure."

Fowler swooped toward the earth and landed in a small clearing near the construction. As Trip rolled off Fowler's back, the giant bird began flapping its wings to take off. "Wait just a minute," Trip said as he lunged for the bird and grabbed for a handful of feathers. "You're not going to leave me here by myself are you?"

"Help you I do not think I can. Remember, 'unlocked it will be by a child's innocent hand'," Fowler answered. Trip clung tight as Fowler began to lift off the ground, but his fingers soon slipped off the oily feathers and he fell to the ground. In less than a minute, Fowler was completely out of sight.

Trip sighed and ran his fingers through his hair as he looked around. He wasn't sure what to do. He felt alone and frightened, but he was also determined to help his friends. He was more determined than he had ever been in his whole life. He found a spot between two trees that had grown closely together and began to plan his next move. From this vantage point, he could observe the stone wall and study the journal, all while being fairly well concealed.

Trip squatted down and leaned against one of the trees and pulled out the leather journal Ben had given him just before the escape. He flipped through the pages until he found the riddle Ben had read to them when they were together in the hideout on the beach. His finger underlined each word as he reread the entry. "A stone message will mark the way, for seafaring ships and where the treasure lay. Two stones to the right and up three blocks, another loose brick will reveal my box."

From where he sat, Trip could just make out the stones that formed the base of the lighthouse. He watched quietly for so long that his legs began to throb from squatting on them. Satisfied that the stones were unguarded, Trip took a deep breath and made his move.

CHAPTER
24
The Ship

Sam, Emily, Susan and Ben sat huddled together on the deck of the huge ship with the menacing looking Jolly Roger flapping loudly above them. It was still dark outside, and the water below looked rough and more black than the night around them.

The children had been untied and left there since their arrival on the ship. When Grimsley reported finding no trace of a coin in the hideout or on any of the children, Bartholomew had made a lot of noise and had threatened them with talk of such things as hangings and walking the plank, but up to this point had done nothing to hurt them. The moment he boarded his ship, Bartholomew began to bark orders at his crew and ordered Grimsley to "take care of the prisoners." Ever since then, the children had sat unnoticed in a corner of the deck near the stern of the vessel.

"Maybe we should try to escape," Sam said.

"How would we do that, Sam?" Emily asked

sarcastically. "Lower that humongous rowboat to the water and row away with oars that all four of us together couldn't dream of lifting? Or how about dive into that black water and swim against the current for who knows how far before we drown?"

"There might be another way," Sam said defensively. "You think of something, Emily. You're the smart one."

Susan looked back and forth between Sam and Emily as the two argued with each other. Emily was just about to attack Sam with another sarcastic barb when she glanced at Susan and saw a crocodile sized tear roll down the girl's cheek. She felt her face get hot with shame and quietly said, "Sorry, Susan. This isn't helping anything."

Ben put his arm around his sister protectively and held her tight. "Let's just wait a little while to see if Trip shows up," he said.

CHAPTER
25

The Box

Trip quickly crossed the clearing to the stones and fell to his knees on the inside of the incomplete, low wall. He examined the rocks, looking for some sort of message. He looked down at Digger's journal and read the riddle for what seemed like the hundredth time.

"A stone message will mark the way, for seafaring ships and where the treasure lay. Two stones to the right and up three blocks another loose brick will reveal my box."

He had almost decided that Ben and Susan had been wrong about the riddle when he spotted a large stone at the bottom of the wall. He hadn't noticed it before because it was partially covered with sand, and even though the moon was bright, it was still dark outside. He leaned over to put his weight on his left hand while he wiped away the sand with his right. As he brushed off the surface of the stone, what he felt with his fingers confirmed what he'd already seen with his eyes. There were letters engraved in the face of the rock.

He finished brushing off the sand and read by moonlight, "The first stone of this beacon was laid on the 30th of May 1767 in the seventh year of His Majesty's Reign, George III."

Trip was disappointed. He had expected a message about the treasure. He sat back on his heels, crossed his arms and read the inscription again. "Well it does say beacon which is a light," he said to himself. "That's good." He looked at the riddle in the journal. "Wait a minute," he thought. "Two stones to the right and up three blocks." He counted two stones past the one with the writing and then counted up. "One, two, three." He put both hands on the stone he had landed on and tried to wiggle it. Sure enough, it moved. There was just enough room for him to squeeze his small fingers in the gaps on either side of the block. He wiggled it back and forth and back and forth over and over again until the heavy stone fell with a thud into the sand in front of him.

Trip stepped up onto the fallen rock and put his face close to the opening in the wall so he could see what was inside, but it was so dark he couldn't see a thing. He cautiously slid his hand back into the hole and felt around for something. His fingers hit what he expected was Digger's box, but it felt bigger than he had thought it would be. He tried to pull it out, but it was too heavy for one hand. He put his other hand in and reached so far back that both arms were in the hole up to his shoulders and his cheek was pressed hard against the cold stone that lay above the hole. He pulled until the box was right at the edge of the opening. There it was. It was Digger's box, but Trip had forgotten to account for his small size. Because Trip was still very small, to him, the box seemed large.

Trip held his breath and slowly released the clasp that held the box closed. He took a quick look around to make sure he was alone and then slowly, he opened the lid. Trip's eyes grew wide as he looked at twelve shiny silver coins inlaid in a bed of plush red velvet. He ran his fingers lightly over the coins. They looked like the drawings in Digger's journal, only more beautiful and intricate in their designs. In the center of the velvet was a shallow round hole that Trip assumed was for the thirteenth coin.

In the lid of the box, there was an inscription that read,

"These coins are magic and transcend
all time.
Travel past and future with help from
this rhyme.
Place number Thirteen in the box and

119

then go

To the top of the lighthouse that will
then itself show.

Once the coins are in place and your
hands on the rail,

This rhyme must be said from the
heart, not the head:

'All of the power that comes with
this treasure,

I'll use it for good and for help
forever'.

Then state the year and the place for
your flight

And away you will go on the beam of
the light."

"But if I do that now, I'll leave everyone else behind," Trip thought. He was excited about having found what he believed to be the treasure, but wasn't sure what to do next. He searched the box for more clues, but didn't see anything else. He closed the box, lifted it with some difficulty and made his way toward the woods. As he struggled with the treasure, Trip felt his sweaty fingers slowly sliding from underneath the bottom of the wooden chest until he lost his grip completely and the box fell to the ground. Trip quickly dropped to his knees to examine the box. He let out a sigh of relief. The lid was still in place, which meant the coins were still safe inside. He decided to drag the box the rest of the way across the clearing toward the trees where he had hidden earlier. He pulled it between the trees and covered it with some loose limbs. Then he picked up a fallen palm frond to brush over the sand. He needed to conceal the tracks he had made while dragging the box. He was anxious to go look for his friends, but decided to check the box one more time to make sure he hadn't damaged it when it fell to the ground. This time he opened the top. He was surprised at what he saw.

The red velvet casing had dislodged and beneath it was a ragged piece of paper. He pulled out the paper, unfolded it and saw a list written there. Trip's eyes scanned over the writing. The numbers one to thirteen were listed down the left-hand side of the paper. Each number had a short description written next to it. Trip skipped down to number thirteen and read, "Auxilium in aqua est" and then "through water help will come for those who believe."

Trip remembered that the Latin words on the 13th coin meant "truth is in water", but this word Auxilium was new to him. He assumed it either had something to do with help or believing. Trip thought about what Grimsley had said to him when he'd let him go. He'd said, "use the coin", hadn't he? He patted his pocket to make sure the 13th coin was still there and began to make his way back toward the ocean.

CHAPTER
26
Help is in Water

By the time Trip made it to the edge of the water, he was exhausted. He was hungry and thirsty and in much need of sleep. But he knew he couldn't stop now. He had to somehow find his friends and get them all back to where the treasure was. He wasn't sure what all the coins could do, but he thought they could get him home, and right now that was the best treasure he could think of.

His mind kept replaying what Grimsley had said. "Use the coin." He heard the phrase repeated over and over again in his brain. He had removed the coin from his pocket and now held it tightly in his sweaty palm. Exhausted, Trip fell to his knees in the surf and held the coin in the ocean. He waved it around in the water and said out loud, "I believe." He looked around expectantly, but nothing happened.

Trip closed his eyes tightly to try to keep back his tears, but there was nothing he could do to stop them. His shoulders began to shake with sobs that came from the depths of his soul. "I don't know what to do!" he yelled at the top of his lungs. "Somebody please help me!" He pulled his arm back, and with all his might, he threw the coin with the flying 13 into the Atlantic Ocean. He regretted it as soon as it left his fingertips. He put his face in his hands and wept even more bitterly.

He didn't look up again until he heard a strange sound. What he saw shocked him. There a few feet in front of him were two huge bottle-nosed dolphins. One of them had Trip's coin in its mouth. The other one made the bleating dolphin noise again and jerked his head toward Bartholomew's ship. It reminded Trip of what a dog does when it wants to be followed. Trip pointed at his own chest and said, "Me? You want me to come with you?"

Both dolphins nodded up and down like Trip had seen dolphins do at a water park his family had visited. He shook his head in disbelief. "Okay," he said. "I've got nothing to lose." Pushing through the surf, he walked toward the dolphins until he couldn't touch the ocean floor with his feet and then he swam the rest of the distance to the enormous sea mammals. He put a hand on the back of the one with the coin and gently took it from the dolphin's mouth. As the animals slowly began to swim, Trip grabbed the leading edge of one of their fins and held on tight.

Within minutes, Trip found himself on the back of one of the giant dolphins looking up at the stern of the large ship.

CHAPTER
27

The Escape

On the ship, Emily, Sam, Ben and Susan still sat huddled together wondering what to do next. It was Susan that heard the bleating of the dolphins first. She peered over the edge to the water below. With her head still hanging over the side she reached back to grab Ben's arm. "Ben, come look at this!" she said. "What is that?"

Ben scooted toward the side and put his head under the railing to get a better look. He couldn't believe his eyes. There was Trip sitting on the back of a dolphin. He was hanging on to the dolphin with one hand and motioning for Ben and the others to jump overboard into the water.

Ben waved so that Trip would know he'd seen him, and then he looked back around to the others. "It's Trip!" Ben said in an excited whisper.

"What do you mean?" Sam said as he scrambled over the others to take a look for himself. As soon as he saw Trip and the dolphins, Sam said, "Yes, I knew it!"

Then he turned toward Emily and said, "Come on smarty pants, time to take a swim." And with that, Sam slipped under the railing, hung on to the edge of the ship for a few seconds and then dropped to the water. Because of the height of the jump, Sam plunged deep into the black ocean. Ben, Susan and Emily watched the surface of the water nervously. They all breathed a collective sigh of relief when Sam's head popped up near the dolphins. He scrambled up onto the dolphin that Trip was riding, looked up at the others and motioned for them to follow.

"You girls go next," Ben said looking back and forth between Susan and Emily. They nodded and climbed to the outside of the railing. They hung there for a few seconds with their heels on the edge of the deck and their arms behind them holding on to the railing. Emily looked at Susan and said, "We can do this." Susan nodded and gave Emily a small smile. Emily grinned back at her and said, "Okay. One, two, three." Both girls uncurled their fingers from the rail and jumped into the dark night and the cool water below.

Ben jerked around to look out across the deck as he heard the loud double splash the girls made. His blood ran cold as he saw Grimsley staring right at him, but the large man hadn't made a move toward him. Up above he heard a voice bellow, "Man overboard!" Ben looked up and saw the source of the voice. High above the deck, a crewman sat perched in the ship's crow's nest. "The prisoners are escaping," he yelled.

Bartholomew, who had just arrived on deck, locked eyes with Ben. Ben quickly turned away, took a step toward the rail, put his hands over his head, and dove through the opening and into the water below. As he rose to the surface, Emily reached out to grab his hand. As soon as Ben was on the back of the second dolphin, the animals raced through the surf carrying the five children toward the beach.

The ship behind them was in total chaos. Men were running everywhere prodded along by Bartholomew's rage. "Lower the rowboats!" he yelled. "Fire the cannon!" "Get them, you lazy dog!" he screamed as he pushed one sailor overboard into the ocean.

The children were nearly to the beach when the first cannonball splashed in the water behind them.

They slid off the backs of the dolphins and swam the last 15 feet to shore. "Thank you!" Emily called to the dolphins. But they had disappeared just as suddenly as they had arrived.

CHAPTER
28

If The Coin Fits

As the children made their way onto the sand, Sam turned around to look in the direction of Bartholomew's ship.

"They've got a rowboat in the water," he warned.

"We better hurry," Trip answered. "They'll be a lot faster than we are."

"Where are we going, Trip?" Ben asked. "Did you find the treasure?"

In all the excitement of the escape, Trip had forgotten that none of the others knew about the treasure. "Yeah, I found it," he said proudly. "I think it's our ticket home."

"Well, where is it?" Ben asked impatiently. "Is it in the foundation of the lighthouse like Susan and I thought?"

"Yeah, you were right," Trip said, "but I moved it to another spot for safekeeping until I could figure out how to get you away from Pickle Breath. Come on, we've got to go. This may be our only chance to get home."

Trip, Sam, Emily, Ben and Susan trudged as quickly as they could through the thick sand and then into the grassy area just beyond the dunes. Once their feet were on more solid ground, all five broke into a full run toward the woods. Just before they ducked into the protective cover of the thick trees, Sam glanced back at the beach behind them. "The rowboat is almost to the beach!" he screamed. "Hurry!"

All five were gasping for breath by the time they reached the round stone wall that was the foundation of the lighthouse, Trip pointed across the small clearing and said, "Over there."

He ran as fast as he could to the spot where he had hidden the large box and quickly pulled away the sticks and leaves that concealed it. "Here it is," he said. "Help me move it over to the wall."

"Why is it so big?" Sam asked.

"It's not that big. We're small. Remember?" Emily answered.

"Oh, right," Sam said.

Ben and Trip each picked up an end of the box, carried it inside the stones and set it in the sand. Trip pointed out the block with the writing on it and where he had found the box. Then he opened the lid and said,

"Look at this," as he pointed to the inscription imprinted on the inside. He read the words aloud.

"These coins are magic and transcend
all time.
Travel past and future with help from
this rhyme.
Place number Thirteen in the box and
then go
To the top of the lighthouse that will
then itself show.
Once the coins are in place and your
hands on the rail,
This rhyme must be said from the
heart, not the head:
'All of the power that comes with
this treasure,
I'll use it for good and for help
forever'.
Then state the year and the place for
your flight
And away you will go on the beam of
the light."

"Do you still have the coin?" Emily asked. In the distance they could hear the angry voices of

Bartholomew and his friends. Trip felt his face get hot with embarrassment as he remembered how he had recklessly thrown the coin into the sea. He didn't have time to explain that now. "Yes, I have it," he answered while he pulled it out of his pocket.

"It's smaller than the other coins," Susan observed. "Do you think it will work?"

The angry voices were getting louder and louder as the men got closer to the round wall and to the children.

"Try it, Trip," Ben urged.

"Hurry, they're coming!" Sam said in a panicky voice.

Trip placed the coin in the spot reserved for the 13th coin. He furrowed his brow and sighed in frustration. Susan was right. It was too small. It must have shrunk along with him and the others when they came here from the year 2006. But as soon as Trip removed his fingers from the coin, a strange glittery mist began to swirl around it. Right before their eyes, the coin expanded to fit snugly in its spot in the velvet lining of the box.

All five children stared in disbelief as the glittery mist began to grow larger and swirl faster. As it began to swirl around them, Susan ran to Ben, wrapped both arms around him and clung to him fiercely. Trip reached out to Emily and Sam and grasped their hands. The faster the mist swirled, the more the wind around them began to blow. The children clung more tightly to each other as their hair and clothes blew wildly in the windy mist.

"Look!" Ben yelled over the volume of the wind. "The lighthouse!"

As the mist swirled around and around, a spiral staircase began to appear right before their eyes. Row by row, the walls of a lighthouse began to appear. The children stared in disbelief. Their mouths dropped open and their eyes grew wide.

An evil laugh behind them startled the children. "The treasure is finally mine!" Bartholomew screamed from the outside of the growing wall. Sam turned to look at him. "He's not big anymore!" Sam exclaimed. Trip looked down at the box. It wasn't big anymore either. Somehow, in the mist, the children had returned to their normal size.

CHAPTER

29

The Lighthouse

"Seize them," Bartholomew bellowed to his men as he pointed at the children. Not a single man made a move toward the lighthouse. They were frozen with fear as they watched the walls begin to build in the strange swirling mist. "What's wrong with you?" he screamed as he pushed a man aside. He ran to the wall, which was growing taller by the second, and began to try and climb over it. When he couldn't, he ran around the outside of the wall looking for some sort of doorway.

Trip leaned down, shut the box and picked it up. The mist continued to swirl around them and more steps appeared before them.

"Up the steps!" Sam yelled.

"They're not real, Sam," Emily exclaimed. "They can't be."

Sam leapt toward the staircase and came down with both feet firm on the first step. He scampered up two more and said, "Feels real to me, let's go!"

With the box tucked securely under his arm, Trip followed his friend up the staircase. Emily, Susan and then Ben followed closely behind. As soon as it would seem they couldn't climb any higher, more steps would appear before them. They could now hear Bartholomew climbing the staircase behind them.

"Hurry, Sam!" Ben called ahead from the back of the line.

"I can't go any faster," Sam answered. He was breathing heavily from climbing the steep staircase. Gasping, Sam made two more turns around the circular stairway and yelled, "I see the top."

As they approached the top of the lighthouse, their nostrils were filled with a strong burning smell. When they reached the top, they saw the source. A container of pitch and tar burned brightly on a platform at the top of the stairs. Around the flame was a polished wooden rail with thirteen coin-sized circles carved in the wood. Below each circle was a Roman Numeral.

Trip balanced the box on the rail and opened the lid.

"Put the coins in their places on the railing," Emily said.

"Yeah, I think that sounds right," Ben added.

Trip began pulling the coins out of the red velvet

casing one at a time. For each one, he would stick his fingernail under the edge of the coin, dislodge it, and hand it to one of his friends to place in its designated spot in the railing. His eyes were watering from the burning tar and they all had sweat dripping down their faces.

He was just about to pry the 13th coin from the box when he heard Sam scream, "Pickle Breath!" Trip looked up to see Bartholomew's sneering face. He stood on the top step of the spiral staircase and held a long curved dagger in his right hand. The children backed away from him as far as possible. Bartholomew looked at them and began to laugh. It started out low and then grew louder and more sinister. "You thought you could outsmart me?" he sneered. The light of the fire reflected on the silver blade of his dagger. "Five little brats? Ha! The power of the treasure belongs to me and nothing will stop me from getting my way."

As he tightened his grasp on his dagger and moved toward the children, a strong hand reached up, grabbed Bartholomew by the ankle and pulled his feet out from under him. He fell hard to the floor. The children pushed themselves closer to the opposite wall from where he lay. The attacker ran the rest of the way up the steps and threw himself on top of Captain Bartholomew.

"Go, before it's too late," the man said in a strained

voice. It was Grimsley.

"I knew it," said Emily. "I knew you were good!"

Grimsley held Bartholomew tightly to the ground. The Captain's cheek was pushed hard on the wooden floor making it difficult for him to speak. A single tear rolled down Grimsley's weathered face, "Don't ever forget old Hula Dog," he said. "Now go."

Trip held the 13th coin in his fist and said, "Everybody hang onto the rail. When I put in the last coin, we're supposed to say this. He repeated part of the rhyme they had read in the box.

"'All of the power that comes with this treasure, I'll use it for good and for help forever.' Then we'll say the year and the place we want to go."

Each child nodded and moved to a spot on the rail. Their hands grasped the smooth surface tightly. "Okay, you ready?"

Bartholomew was trying his hardest to escape Grimsley's hold, but the larger man easily overpowered the Captain. Sam, Emily, Ben and Susan all watched Trip put the box on the ground, grasp the rail with his left hand and with his right hand carefully place the 13th coin in its' spot on the rail. "Okay, now," he said.

In unison, all five children repeated the rhyme. "All of the power that comes with this treasure, I'll use it for good and for help forever." Then, at the same time the Millers said 1986, Trip, Sam and Emily yelled out 2006. Then they all screamed, "Mount Pleasant, South Carolina."

The glittery mist grew thicker, swirled around the children and lifted them from where they were standing. They all began to slide down the beam of light cast from the height of the lighthouse and then, they disappeared.

CHAPTER

30

Coming Home

Trip never let go of Sam and Emily as they swirled in the strange mist and then slid down the beam of light. He wasn't sure what happened next, but before he knew it, he and his two friends landed with a thud in the lush grass of a well-manicured lawn. He looked down at his hands and saw that his knuckles were white from squeezing his friends' hands. He slowly released his grip and looked at Sam and then Emily.

"You okay?" he asked. He was surprised at how shaky his voice sounded. They both nodded their heads that they were, but Trip was unconvinced that they had recovered quite yet. He knew he hadn't.

"Whoa," Sam said. "That was intense."

"Where are the Millers?" Emily asked looking around and then added, "Where are we?" As she glanced behind where she was sitting she said, "Is that our well?" She stood up to get a closer look. There engraved in the top of the well were the words, "To set it free you must let go, time will fly, away you'll go." Emily ran her fingertips over the words as she read them.

"It is," she said pointing at the inscription. "Look."

Trip and Sam got up and walked over to the well. They heard the sound of a horn honking in the distance and the beeping of a garbage truck backing up. Trip noticed the noises and felt relief wash over him. Noises like that must mean that they were no longer visitors in a past century.

"Huh," he said thoughtfully. "But if that's the well, this would have to be the Old Miller place." He looked around at the beautiful lawn with beds full of blooming flowers and at the perfectly maintained home with wide sweeping porches.

"You think it could be?" Sam asked.

"Maybe," Emily added.

About that time, Trip, Sam and Emily saw a man and a woman running toward them. The people were waving and had big grins on their faces.

"Should we run?" Sam asked.

"I don't think so," Emily said. "They look friendly."

"I wonder who they are?" Trip added.

When the adults got closer, the man said, "You

made it! I knew you would, but it seemed like it would never happen."

Trip looked at the man questioningly.

The woman approached Emily and gave her a big hug. "I wouldn't have made it without you, Emily. I've thought of you so often. Thank you."

Emily awkwardly patted the woman on the back as she accepted her embrace.

The man studied the confused looks on the children's faces and said, "Susan, I don't think they know who we are."

"Oh, I'm sorry," she said, taking a step back from Emily.

"Trip, Sam, Emily, it's us, Ben and Susan Miller," the man said with an amused grin. "We made it back to 1986. But we weren't expecting you to show up until this year."

The children's eyes grew wide. "Wow!" Sam said. "You're grown-ups."

Susan laughed and said, "Yes, but we're still kids at heart."

"Weren't you really just kids a few minutes ago?" Sam asked, confused.

"Probably were to you," Ben answered. "That's the strange thing about time travel, it's not bound by time.

We came back to the same day and place we had left in 1986. No one even missed us this time."

"Thanks to you," Susan added.

Trip looked around him on the ground. "Well, where's the treasure? Do you have it?"

"When we first arrived back home, we didn't know what had happened to it," Ben explained. "But it didn't take long for us to realize that all of the coins were close by."

"The coins were all in our pockets," Susan added. "Can you believe that?"

Trip nodded his head. "Yeah, I'd believe just about anything."

"Have you used the coins?" Emily asked.

"That's another story for another time," Susan said. "You should get home before your families begin to worry."

"Let's just say, you've got a lot to learn about the treasure," Ben said. "You've only just begun to understand its potential."

The children weren't in the mood to argue now. They were famished, exhausted and most of all glad to be home. They agreed to meet the Millers here again the following Saturday.

"Come on, guys," Trip said, "Let's go home."

He put one arm around Emily's shoulders and his other around Sam's.

Sam shook his head in disbelief. "No one would ever believe this even if we told them," he said.

"At least *we* all know we're not crazy," Emily said with a laugh.

When they turned to leave, Ben called, "Oh, wait a minute. I almost forgot. I believe these belong to you." He handed Sam a white trash bag.

Sam opened it up, looked inside and grinned. "It's your backpack, Trip," Sam said. "And look at this," he said, pulling something out of the bag. "You found my shoe." Sam leaned over, pulled his worn shoe over his tattered sock, and arm in arm the three friends walked toward home.